PRAISE FOR CATHERINE ASARO

"Asaro's Skolian saga is now nearly as long and in many ways as compelling as *Dune*, if not more so, featuring a multitude of stronger female characters."
—*Booklist*

"Asaro plants herself firmly into that grand SF tradition of future history franchises favored by luminaries like Heinlein, Asimov, Herbert, Anderson, Dickson, Niven, Cherryh, and Baxter. It really seems to me that any future mention of this stefnal lineage must include her name as a worthy exemplar." —*Locus*

"Catherine Asaro's Saga of the Skolian Empire may be the most important and entertaining science fiction series to originate in the 1990s." —Cynthia Ward, author of *The Adventure of the Golden Woman*

"Asaro's portrait of interstellar intrigue, weird socio-political customs and galactic history has come to approach the neighborhood of such classics as Frank Herbert's *Dune* series." —*Booklist*

THE
SPACETIME
POOL

THE SPACETIME POOL

CATHERINE ASARO

OPEN ROAD
INTEGRATED MEDIA
NEW YORK

This edition published in 2022 by Open Road Integrated Media, Inc.
180 Maiden Lane
New York, NY 10038
www.openroadmedia.com

THE
SPACETIME
POOL

INTRODUCTION

"The Spacetime Pool" first appeared in the March 2008 issue of *Analog* magazine as the cover story. It was later reprinted in the hardcover anthology *Aurora in Four Voices,* which was put out by ISFiC Press for my Guest of Honor appearance at the 2011 Windycon convention.

The story was nominated for the Nebula Award® in a year when I was unable to attend the ceremony due to previous commitments. The night the awards were given, I was sitting in my bedroom, wishing I could be there. On a whim, I went to Twitter and searched on "SFWA" or "Nebula Award." I don't recall exactly what I looked for, but what I found was unexpected; a live feed from the ceremony. Startled, I read the tweets. They were announcing an award that came early in the ceremony. So I waited, knowing it would be a while before they reached novella.

Then suddenly, out of order, a tweet came with the winner for novella.

"The Spacetime Pool."

It was one of my best online moments. I couldn't be present to accept the award, but I could share that moment with my friends through a wireless universe that not so many years ago seemed as much like science fiction as the stories we write. I posted on my Facebook about the win and friend after friend responded until my wall was filled with comments. Instead of sitting wistfully alone in my room late at night, I was suddenly part of a community that shared that wonderful moment.

It meant the world to me.

1

APPALACHIA

The hiker vanished.

Janelle peered at the distant hill. She could have sworn a person had appeared there—and disappeared just as fast. Perhaps it was a trick of the wind. The rhododendron bushes on the hillside where she sat undulated in the breezes like a dark ocean frothed with purple flowers, and a hum of cicadas filled the air. The Great Smoky Mountains rose in the distance, green and gray against a late afternoon sky as blue as a cerulean glaze.

She shifted her weight, wondering if she should have come out here alone. Her hair blew across her face in a swirl that reminded her of yellow corn in the fields back home. The breeze whispered against her arms and rippled the summer dress she had worn instead of sensible hiking clothes. Right now she probably resembled some forest creature more than a new college graduate. She smiled at the image that conjured up: Janelle the wild-woman stalking into math class, strewing leaves and equations. Then her disquiet returned, like a hawk gliding in the sky, circling a rabbit, ready to plunge.

"Oh, stop," she muttered, annoyed at herself. She pulled her hair out of her face. Birds wheeled above the figure on the next ridge—

Someone *was* there. She strained to see better. A man was standing on that hill with his back to her. As she rose to her feet, he turned in her direction.

Then he compressed into a line and vanished.

Whoa. Seriously? Janelle squinted at the hill. She must have mistaken whatever she had seen. She had no wish to share her solitude, but curiosity tugged at her. She hiked up the hill and headed back to the trail, uncertain whether to investigate the vanished fellow or return to her car. Although it would take thirty minutes to reach the parking lot, she should probably go back; the afternoon had cooled as it aged, and her flimsy dress couldn't stave off the chill. Seeking an escape from her hectic life, she had left her cell phone and purse in the car, taking nothing more than her keys.

The leafy canopy of an old growth forest arched above her. Wood chips crackled under her feet, and a red squirrel skittered up the trunk of a basswood. Stretching out her arms, she turned in a circle, her eyes closed. Sweet blazes, she loved these mountains. Laughing, she opened her eyes. Life was good. She had finished her math degree at MIT a few days ago and it felt great.

Like a shift in a sea current, her mood changed. She had no one to share her happiness. It had been two years since her father's assassination in Spain. Her mother and brother had unexpectedly joined him for lunch that day, and the explosion that destroyed his car had taken them as well, her entire family. Even now, the pain felt raw.

Janelle inhaled deeply. She would survive this moment, as she had all the others, until the grief became bearable.

"Janelle?" a voice asked.

What that. . . ? She whirled around.

A man stood several paces away. He resembled the guy from the hill, though she hadn't seen him well enough to be sure this was the same person. She stepped back. He had only said her name, but given that they had never met, that was plenty to make her nervous.

His presence did nothing to reassure her. He was too tall, maybe six foot six, with a muscular physique. His clothing was strange. She had nothing against unconventional self-expression, but in some not-so-subtle way, this went beyond that. The blue of his shirt vibrated in the shadowed forest, as vivid as an ocean where sunlight slanted through the water. His black pants were tucked into black boots. Silver links set with abalone gleamed on his shirt cuffs and in the silver chain around his neck. Well-trimmed hair brushed his shoulders, glossy and black. It wasn't the length that surprised her, but the grey at the temples. Although obviously hale and fit, he seemed rather old to adopt such styles. Then again, just because she knew no one his age who made that kind of fashion statement, that didn't mean it never happened.

What compelled her the most, though, was his face. His high cheekbones and strong nose, and the dark brows arching above his gray eyes, made her think of a Senator in the Roman Empire. He projected a sense of contained force.

Then she saw what hung from his belt. Ah, hell. *Dagger* was too tame a word. The sheath for the knife stretched as long as her forearm.

"I didn't mean to startle you." His gravelly voice had an unfamiliar accent, harsh and throaty. "You are Janelle Aulair, aren't you?"

She stood poised to run. "Why do you want to know?"

"I was sent to look for you."

With relief, she realized what must have happened. Ben, the grocer in town, had sent him to check on her. Ben always worried when she came up here alone. The last time he had sent his sister and brother-in-law, and they had spooked her the same way.

"Have we met?" She thought she would remember someone so striking, but maybe not.

"Never." Then he added, "Destiny requires your presence," as if that explained everything.

Destiny indeed. She should get back to her car. He hadn't threatened her, but if that changed, she could surely outrun someone his age. She stepped to the side—

"No, wait!" he said, lunging forward.

Startled, she jumped away—

Darkness enveloped Janelle, muffled and cold. Muted voices echoed, calling, fading. Then the light brightened. She stumbled on the sand and barely caught her balance.

Sand?

She looked up—and froze.

2

THE RIEMANN GATE

A white beach stretched around Janelle, dazzling in the bright day. Waves crashed a few yards away and their swells glinted in the slanting rays from the sun, which was low in the sky. The ocean stretched to the horizon, wide, blue, and endless.

"What the blazes?" Janelle spun around—

In time to see the man appear out of thin air.

He came out of nothing, taking a long step. His progress was slowed to a surreal speed, and his body flickered as if he were a projection of light. It *couldn't* be real. He had to be doing this with mirrors. Either that, or she had overworked herself in school more than she realized, and her mind was lodging a protest by wigging out.

The man solidified. For a moment he just stood, squinting at her, looking as disoriented as she felt. The large tendons in his neck corded under the chain he wore, and the sun caught gleams from the abalone. The metal looked like real silver. The contrast of his powerful build with the jewelry unsettled her; no guy she knew wore a necklace, especially not a man this daunting. It wasn't right or wrong, just eerily *different*.

"Are you all right?" he asked.

What a question. Her heart rate had ratcheted up and her head was swimming. "Is this a movie set?" If he had equipment to create this illusion, she should have seen it, but she grasped at the possibility like a swimmer clutching at driftwood in the ocean.

"A moving set? Whatever that is, no." He rested his hand on the hilt of his knife and scanned the area. "Did anyone see you?"

She glanced at the knife, then at his face. "I don't want trouble."

"Nor do I." He stepped toward her. "We shouldn't stay here."

She stepped back. "Why? Where is this? What happened to the mountains?"

He spoke carefully, as if she were breakable and his words were hammers. "They are elsewhere." He indicated a line of straggly trees up the beach, where the sand met a sparse forest. "We must go. We will be safer if we aren't in plain view."

"Safer from what?" She wasn't going anywhere with him.

"Raiders." He scanned the beach, poised as if he were ready to fight. Wind blew his hair back from his face, accenting his prominent nose and strong chin. His profile looked like it belonged on a coin. "We must leave before they come."

"Hey, I'll just go home," she said.

He turned toward her and she was acutely aware of his height. Large men rattled her. They lived in another dimension, one where you could use the top of bookcases and see over the heads of a crowd. They loomed, and he was doing it much too well.

"I'm not sure you can," he said. "This last time, I barely made it through before the gate closed."

"What gate?" Sweat was gathering on her palms. "Who *are* you?"

"You may call me Dominick."

"Yeah, well, what do you want with me, Dominick?"

"You are part of a prophecy." He spoke as if that were a perfectly reasonable statement. "Before my brother or I was born, it was foretold that whichever of us married you would kill the other."

Marriage and murder. Right. She should have listened to Ben and not gone hiking alone. "Don't play with me." Her voice cracked on the last word.

His strong features softened unexpectedly. "I am sorry. I didn't really expect the gate to open."

"My friends are waiting for me." She was talking too fast. "If I don't show up, they'll phone the police." In truth, no one expected her for days. But he didn't know that. She hoped.

"I don't know what is phone," he said. "But we *must* go." He strode forward.

As Janelle whirled to run, the sand shifted under her feet and she tripped. Dominick easily caught her. Twisting in his grip, she raked his arm with her fingernails, and the two of them nearly fell into the sand. He ended up swinging her in a circle with one arm around her waist. He wrapped the other arm around her torso, pinning her while he bent over to hold her in place. He felt as if he were built from iron. She struggled and he tightened his hold.

"Janelle, listen." He spoke urgently. "I won't hurt you. But if we stay here, we could be killed. Outlaws have been raiding homesteads in this area. You're a beautiful woman. If they find you with no defense except me, you would be in far worse trouble than you think I might cause. And I would be dead."

She didn't want to listen. But she had to do something. What if he was telling the truth? What if he *wasn't*? If she made the wrong choice, one or both of them could end up dead.

"Janelle?" he asked.

She took a deep breath. "All right." *For now.*

He grasped her upper arm and set off for the trees. She had to run to keep up with his long-legged stride. So much for hoping age would slow him down. His large hand engulfed her arm in a grip that could have bruised, but he didn't let it. The contrast between the contained violence of his personality and his careful touch confused her.

The fine-grained sand showed little trace of their progress. They soon reached the forest and strode under its sparse cover. They plunged into the deepening woods, keeping up the grueling pace until a stitch burned in her side.

Dominick angled through a tangle of bushes into a denser knot of trees. As they pushed through the bushes, he used his knife to cut away branches. The thicker foliage screened them from view, but it wasn't until they reached the center of the glade that he slowed down. He motioned her toward a boulder that jutted up to about waist height. Sitting on another, he planted his boots on the ground, braced his palms on his knees, and heaved in large breaths. Janelle stayed on her feet, too nervous to sit as she struggled to catch her wind.

"We can rest here," he said as his breathing settled.

She rubbed her arms, feeling cold despite the heat. It was much warmer than in the Smoky Mountains, and she didn't want to dwell on the implications of that fact. "I don't understand how you know me."

"Only through the prophecy." He watched her as if she were the apparition rather than this entire place. "I didn't really expect to find you."

"How do you know I'm the right person?"

"You look like the vision in the Jade Pool. It's near a mountain lodge where my father took his seeress." Sarcasm edged his voice. "Apparently she made better predictions when she was alone with him in secluded retreats."

Right. Father of the year. Choosing tact, she said only, "What did she predict?"

He considered her. "Just days before my mother gave birth for the first time, the seeress showed my father a vision of you. She said Maximillian and I would be his oldest sons, that whichever of us married you would kill the other, and that if either of us tried to kill you, that brother would die."

"That's horrible."

Dryly he said, "My parents weren't delighted with it." He studied her face. "The scribes copied your image from the pool. But you are much younger than the woman in those portraits."

"I doubt they were pictures of me."

"It's more than appearance," he said. "The gate was supposed to bring me to you. It took me three tries today to get it right, but this time it actually worked. And the seeress knew your name. Janelle Aulair."

"You could have looked me up on the Internet."

"What is the Internet?"

Like he didn't know. Maybe next he would try to sell her swampland in Florida. "It's not important. Just tell me how to get back home."

He dropped his hand to his belt and set his palm over a disk. It differed from the abalone circles on his clothes; this one had a metallic sheen. He stared at the ground, his gaze unfocused.

"Dominick?" she asked.

He looked up at her. "The gate doesn't open."

She pushed back her growing fear. "That's convenient."

"It's true." He ran his fingers over the disk. "Do you feel anything?"

"Nothing."

"I'm trying to create the gate where you're standing."

She didn't know what to think. "How did you learn to use it?"

"One of the monks told me."

Now they had monks, too. What next? "How did he find out?"

"I don't know."

"A description has to be somewhere. Books, files, storage."

He seemed oddly bewildered. "You mean a library?"

"Yes!" If they had web service there, she could contact someone for help.

"I have one at my home," he said.

The last place she wanted to go was his house. "A public library would be better."

"I don't know what that is."

She couldn't believe him. That he sounded perfectly sane didn't help any. "And you have no idea how this gate works?" she challenged.

His gaze flashed. "Of course I do. It's a branch. From here to your mountains."

"A tree, you mean?"

"No. A branch cut to another page. Your universe is one sheet, mine is another."

She gaped at him. "Do you mean a *Riemann sheet*? A branch cut from one Riemann sheet to another?"

"That's right." He hesitated. "You know these words?"

She laughed unsteadily. "It's nonsense. Not the sheets, I mean, but they're just mathematical constructs! They don't actually exist. You can't physically go *through* a branch cut any more than you could step under a square root sign."

He was watching her with a skeptical expression that mirrored how she had felt when he told her about his prophecy. "I have no idea what you're talking about."

"Complex variable analysis." She felt as if she were in a play where she only knew part of the script. "A branch cut is like a slit in a sheet of paper. It opens onto another sheet. I suppose you could say the sheets are alternate universes. But they aren't real."

"They seem quite real," he said. "When you went through the gate, it threw off my calibration. I had set it to come out at my camp." More to himself than to her, he added, "I hadn't actually expected to *leave* the camp."

"Tell you what," Janelle said. "How about you and your brother find wives here? I'll just drop out of the picture." She thought of what he had said about his father. "Unless you're already married. Because if this is all some story for you to get a little fun on the side, forget it."

"Neither Maximillian nor I are wed. I have had concubines, though not in some years."

"Concubines!"

He grinned. "You don't like that?"

Just like a guy, to be pleased when he thought she was jealous. "Oh, honestly, cut that sexist business."

He had the audacity to look intrigued. "What does 'sexist' mean? Is it to do with love-making?"

She glared at him. "No. It means I should go back to Tennessee."

His voice softened. "This world would much poorer, to lose such beauty as yours."

"Don't." For some reason, it angered her that he actually sounded sincere with that line. Or maybe the anger masked her fear. Right now, he could do whatever he wanted with her.

"My brother Max wouldn't give you a choice." He was no longer smiling. "If not for the prophecy that we would die if we killed you, he would probably execute you on sight."

An unwelcome memory jumped into her mind: she had learned about the deaths of her family from a television broadcast. Someone with too much ambition and too little compassion had leaked the story, sensationalizing it as an "execution." Janelle had been visiting a girlfriend in Virginia during a school break, and the news had gone public even as government officials scrambled to find her.

Dominick spoke quietly. "Your face looks like a dark cloud passed over it."

She shook her head, unable to answer.

"I do regret all this." He stood up and lifted his hand, inviting her to leave the glade. "Are you rested enough to go on? Let me at least bring you to my home, as my honored guest."

Janelle didn't want to be his guest. But she was beginning to absorb that this might be real, and hanging around in this glade didn't seem likely to bring her home.

The sun was setting when they emerged from the bushes. The world had darkened and blurred, as if they saw it through old glass on the seashore, brown and rounded by tumbling waves.

Dominick set off along a faint path scattered with leaves. They had only gone a few yards, however, when he paused, listening. Then he spoke in an urgent whisper. "*Run.*"

She took one look at his face—and broke into a sprint.

3

THE TRANSFORM PALACE

Janelle raced through the woods, and Dominick's boots thudded behind her. Then she tripped on a jutting rock, and he plowed into her. Holding her around the waist with one arm, he lurched past a tangle of wild berry bushes and fell behind a large boulder and the bushes. He twisted in mid-air and landed on his back, cushioning their fall so she came down on top of him. It all happened so fast, her breath went out in a rush. For one second, he held her in a vise-like embrace, staring at her face, so close she could see the gold lines in the green irises of his eyes.

Dominick sat up fast, rolling her off his body and onto her stomach. She pushed up on her hands, but when he laid his palm on her back, she stopped with her head raised. He crouched next to her, his knife drawn, his head tilted as if he were listening to the distant waves. Her surge of adrenalin sharpened her hearing, and she caught the shushing of hooves on sand. Dominick raised his dagger in a single sure motion, the blade glinting in the dying rays of the sun.

Hooves stamped nearby. Janelle stayed silent, though surely they could hear the thud of her heart, it was so like thunder in her own ears. Voices spoke in a patois of heavily accented English sprinkled with unfamiliar words. Straining to understand, she just barely made out that they were talking about the "two on the beach," that they would finish off the man and take the girl. When she heard what they wanted to do with her, bile rose in her throat.

The voices moved away until only the shush of waves on the beach broke the evening's silence. Dominick spoke under his breath, no words she recognized, what sounded like an oath. She breathed out, suddenly aware of her rigid posture.

"I think we can go," Dominick said in a low voice.

Janelle was finally absorbing that she might truly be stranded in this violent place with no anchor except this stranger. "I can't," she whispered.

"It will work out." Despite his rough voice, he had a kind tone. "Come with me, Janelle. I will do well by you."

Get a grip, she told herself. Taking a breath, she climbed to her feet. "I'm all right." She wished it were true.

Dominick had stood with her. He lifted his hand as if to touch her face, but when she tensed, he lowered his arm.

They set off again, and the ocean's mumble receded as they ventured deeper among the trees. The woods thickened into a heavy forest and tufts of wild grass stuck up in the soil. Dusk came like a great beast, one barely noticed until it spread its wings, darkening every copse and glade. Luminescent bottle flies hummed among the trees.

Dominick drew her to a stop. Holding his fingers to his mouth, he gave a whistle that rose and fell in an eerie tune. A bird answered his call.

"Hai," a low voice said.

Janelle started. A man had appeared under a nearby tree. He wore leather armor and a dagger similar to Dominick's, but without silver or abalone inlaid in its hilt. He also had an "extra" that made her mouth go dry, a monstrous broadsword strapped across his back with its hilt sticking above his shoulders.

Dominick spoke in the same dialect used by the men who wanted to kill him. It sounded like, "Hava moon strake camp," but she thought he meant, "Have the men strike camp." Although she didn't understand the other man's response, she saw the deference in his bow. The man glanced at her with curiosity, then withdrew into the trees and vanished as silently as he had come.

When Dominick tried to take her arm, she stepped away from him with a start. He didn't pressure her; instead, he lifted his hand as if he were inviting her to his world. Wary, she continued on with him. Although she saw no one else, she didn't think they were alone anymore.

They soon entered a clearing of trampled grass. Several tents stood on the far side, and men moved in the trees beyond, soldiers it looked like, in leather armor. Most were tending animals. Their mounts resembled horses, but with tufts for tails. Each of the animals had two horns, one on either side of its head, with the tips pointing inward. Some of the men wore helmets with similar horns. The scene had a dreamlike quality, all in the dusk with mist curling around the trees. But the cooling air on her arms and legs and the pungent smell of wet grass were all too real.

The men greeted Dominick with respect. Although Janelle had trouble deciphering their words, she understood their intent. They were preparing to leave.

And she was going with them.

Fog muffled the night. Janelle sat in front of Dominick on one of the two-horned animals, which he called a biaquine and had named Starlight for its silver coat. He changed its saddle to a tasseled blanket woven in heavy red and white yarn so Janelle could more easily sit with him. A few scouts rode on ahead, but the rest of the men stayed together, with extra biaquines to carry the tents and other supplies. Fear and curiosity warred within Janelle. She had agreed to go with Dominick because she saw no other viable choices, at least not where she stayed alive and healthy. But she didn't trust him.

They passed through veils of mist, climbing into the mountains. Her muscles ached from the unfamiliar ride. Moonlight lightened the fog, and she strove to keep track of landmarks that loomed out of the night: a gnarled tree with two trunks, a cracked stone overhang looming above the path, a weathered statue of an elderly man in a niche of rock. Her ties to home were growing tenuous, unable to compete with the reality of this impossible place.

Dominick put his arms around her waist so she didn't fall off the biaquine. At first she sat ramrod straight in his hold. Gradually, though, Starlight's rocking gait lulled her. Nor did Dominick pressure her in any way. She had forgotten how comforting it felt just to be held. Her mother had always been effusive with affection, and although her father had been less demonstrative, he had never let them doubt his love. She had grown up secure in those close-knit ties. One instant of violence had shattered everything. Drowning in grief, she had withdrawn from human contact, and in the two years since she had barely touched another person.

"Janelle," Dominick said after a while. "I have a request."

"A request?" She mentally shook herself out of her half-trance. "What do you mean?"

"I would like a curl of your hair."

"My hair? Why?"

"It is important."

She waited, but when he said no more, she decided it wasn't worth pressing the point. So she said, "All right."

He moved one arm away from her waist, and the scrape of metal against leather grated behind her. Startled, she stiffened and was about to turn around when his arm came around her again—with his long dagger, its hilt clenched in his fist.

Janelle froze, her gaze riveted on the blade as it glittered in the moonlight. "What are you doing?" she asked, hating the tremor in her voice.

"Just this." Dominick carefully cut of a tendril of her hair. He gave it to one of his riders, who was cantering next to them. The man placed the strands in a packet of cloth and then took off up the trail, galloping ahead of their party.

Janelle didn't speak until she heard Dominick sheath his knife again. Then she asked, "What will he do with it?"

"My monks will examine it," Dominick said. "To see if you are who I think."

"How can they know from a lock of hair?"

"They have . . . spells."

"Spells?"

"Well," he amended. "So they say."

From his tone, she suspected he didn't believe it any more than she did. She just hoped his monks didn't decide her hair had demonic properties.

Exhaustion was catching up to her, but she was afraid to rest, dreading what she might find when she awoke. She had rarely slept enough during school, often studying late into the night. She had earned high marks, even the top grade in her class on mathematical methods of physics, but now her pleasure in a job well done seemed forlorn.

An owl hooted, its call muted by the fog. Janelle shuddered.

"Are you cold?" Dominick asked.

"I was thinking of home."

Regret softened the edges of his voice. "I am sorry about this." After a pause, he added, "But I would be lying if I denied I am glad you are here. I never really believed this would happen."

"Prophecies aren't real." She watched the biaquines plodding ahead of them on the trail. "A rational explanation has to exist."

"Truthfully?" he said. "I don't think the seeress made that prediction. It was Gregor, a monk from the monastery. He is the one who can read the Jade Pool." His gravelly voice scraped the air. "Father's soothsayer had never even been there before. She stayed at the palace."

"Palace?"

"Where my brother is."

"Does he work there?"

He gave a bitter laugh. "You could say that."

"What does he do?"

"He is the Emperor of Othman."

Oh. Sure. Hey, an emperor. She didn't know which would be more disturbing, if he was crazy or if he were telling the truth. "You're the brother of an emperor?"

"Yes." He said it simply, just verifying a fact. "He was born first."

If neither he nor his brother had married, that suggested neither had legitimate offspring. "Does that mean you're his heir?"

"For now. Until he sires one."

"Sweet blazes," she said in a low voice. "I've never heard of Othman."

He swept out his hand as if to show her all the land. "The provinces stretch from the snow fields of the far north to the great gulf in the south. Maximillian rules it all and I govern the Atlantic Province under him."

"He has the entire continent?" It sounded like Canada and North America.

"Only the eastern half. Britain has the rest." In a deceptively soft voice, he added, "For now."

"And later?"

"That depends on what happens with Max."

From his tone, she had little doubt that if he became emperor, he would kick out the British and conquer their territories. What a strange history for the colonial revolution.

"Your brother is afraid you're after his throne," she said.

"Supposedly, whichever of us marries you will rule Othman."

"This is crazy. I have nothing to do with either of you."

"Not according to the seer."

Or the politicians, more likely. "Dominick, surely you see this so-called prophecy is a trick, one guaranteed to set you and your brother against each other. It's bunk."

"Bunk?"

"Lies. Moonshine."

"Moonshine." He gave a wry laugh. "An apt image."

Janelle wished she hadn't used the word. It evoked faded memories of her southern childhood: grits, biscuits and gravy, and bluegrass music. Her family had later moved to Washington, D.C. and then Spain, but inside she was still that girl who loved country ham and the unique twang of a steel guitar. Her memories glimmered with images of the golden hills she had wandered during late summer days, spinning the enchanted dreams of youth. She couldn't let herself think that she might never again see them.

"I would agree that it is 'moonshine,'" Dominick was saying. "Except everything else in the prophecy has come true. It foretold the birth of eight children to my parents. Max and I have six siblings, and they fit every detail predicted." His breath condensed in the air, spuming past her. "Gregor gave my father a sealed letter, to be opened after father's death. Father died of pneumonia ten years ago, three days after his sixtieth birthday. After the funeral, Maximillian opened the letter."

"What did it say?"

He answered quietly. "That my father would die of pneumonia three days after his sixtieth birthday."

She shivered. "That's eerie."

"Indeed."

"You and Maximillian can never trust each other."

"True. Not that I would trust him anyway."

"Why not?"

"He craves power."

She didn't doubt that also applied to Dominick. "Why are you so certain it's me in that prophecy? You've only seen drawings of an older woman."

"We will verify your signature."

"You've never seen me write, I'm sure."

"Not writing." He paused. "It's hard to explain."

Right. "Try."

"Your signature is supposed to be inside your body. It has forty-six characters, half each from your father and your mother. You can't see it, I think because it is too small." He nuzzled the top of her head. "It determines everything about you, from the color of your eyes to whether you are a man or a woman."

The touch of his lips on her hair startled Janelle. It was a simple gesture, but that just made it more intimate, as if they took such affections for granted. Attractive he might be, but so were a lot of people, and she didn't let them kiss her hair either. She started to tell him to stop, then stopped when she realized what else he had said. The "signature" sounded like DNA. Based on what she had seen, she wouldn't have expected his people to know genetics at the molecular level needed to identify a person. Then she gave a frayed laugh. She didn't believe they understood DNA, but she accepted gates to other universes?

He spoke stiffly. "What is funny?"

Belatedly, she realized how her reaction must sound. "Dominick, I wasn't laughing at—" She foundered on the word "kiss," which felt too awkward, and wasn't exactly what he had done, anyway. So she told another truth. "I'm tired. Nervous." Softly, she added, "Don't push."

"It is true, this was all ill prepared." After a moment, he added, "I have never before used the gate."

"You must have studied it." How else could he have found her?

He shook his head, or at least his hair rustled behind her. "I just use the tools Gregor gave me," he said.

"The disk on your belt."

"Yes. Except apparently now it no longer does anything."

"Maybe I can get it to work."

She expected him to refuse her permission to try. Instead, he took his arm away from her waist, and she heard a click. Then he pressed the metal plate he had showed her earlier into her hand. It had a diameter the size of her palm and felt cool on her skin. No marks embellished its polished surface.

"How does it operate?" she asked.

"I rub it. Supposedly my finger ridges activate the spells."

Spells indeed. If his fingerprints operated the mechanism, it wouldn't work for her. When she rubbed the disk, nothing happened. "Should I touch it in any pattern?"

"Not that I know of."

"You said before that you had calibrated it."

"Actually, Gregor is the one who set it up. He's secretive. He tells me nothing." Wryly he added, "I don't think he understands it, either." He guided Starlight around an outcropping, and the biaquine snorted as if to protest the inconvenience. Then Dominick said, "What you told me about 'sheets' earlier. What did you mean?"

She handed him back the disk. "It's kind of abstruse."

He snorted. "Does that mean you don't know?"

"No," she growled, irked. "Imagine one Riemann sheet as my universe. It has a phase."

"Like the moon."

"Not that." She paused, thinking. "Do you have clocks here?"

"Well, yes. Certainly."

"Twenty-four hours a day? Twelve and twelve again?"

"Of course."

It relieved her that she at least had that much in common with him. "Think of the phase as time. Say it goes from midnight to noon in my universe." She almost said "like hands on an old-fashioned clock," but then realized analog timepieces were probably the norm here rather than in danger of becoming relics of an earlier age, like in her universe.

"And my world is the second clock?" Dominick asked. "Time goes from noon to midnight here?"

"Yes!" He understood fast. That boded well, she hoped.

"The time here and where I found you was the same," he said.

"I know. I don't mean my world and yours are literally related by a twelve-hour difference. Just that they're in some way out of phase with each other, like three in the morning is different than three in the afternoon, even though they're called the same thing."

He was quiet for a while. Then he said, "So this 'branch cut' to your universe is located at a certain phase. It's like saying the gate opens only at a certain time."

"That would be my guess."

"To go around this metaphorical clock and return to the branch cut must take longer than twelve hours. The disk never worked before."

"How long have you been trying?"

"Over forty years. Since I was very small."

Forty! That wasn't what she wanted to hear. "Every *day*?"

"Actually, no." He sounded embarrassed. "I should have been trying more often. Max did more than me, and we've both put more effort into the whole matter as we've grown older, with the pressure to settle this and produce heirs. But it just all seems so fanciful." Dryly he added, "Seemed."

No kidding. At least if he didn't always check, he could have missed the gate. She hoped that was why he hadn't found her before this. Or she could be wrong about the whole thing. "I need to read about the theory."

"Such studies are for monks." He sounded surprised.

Janelle had no objection to being considered monkish if it would get her home. Perhaps what she lacked in savvy about this world she could make up for in her ability to solve problems. "Do you have books about the gates?"

"In my library."

"Maybe I can learn to make a gate." Or find a more logical explanation.

"If it pleases you to look, you may."

She wondered if reading would be a problem. "But Dominick."

He bent his head, bringing his lips to her ear. His breath tickled the sensitive skin there. "Hmmm?"

"Oh." She forgot what she had been about to say. His scent surrounded her, a combination of saffron, thyme and sweat. She was suddenly conscious of how close they were sitting on the biaquine.

He spoke against her ear. "I like your hair. You look like a forest sprite." He brushed his lips across her cheek.

"Stop." She was almost stuttering.

He let out a breath. But he lifted his head and straightened up. The night air cooled her cheek.

"What did you wish to ask me?" he asked, his tone more formal.

"Your speech." She wasn't certain what unsettled her more, his kiss or that she had liked it. "When you speak to your men, you don't use English."

"Yes I do."

"What do you call what we're speaking?"

"Erst. No one uses it anymore." His voice lightened. "As a youth I complained greatly about having to learn a dead language. I'm glad now that I did."

"It's not dead to me." She hoped.

"Then I am gratified I know it."

"Tell me something," she said. "Why didn't you expect to find me?"

"I guess I assumed that if you existed, it would lead naturally to your coming here. I didn't think it would happen by mistake *only* because I looked for you."

She rubbed her eyes. "Talk about a self-fulfilling prophecy."

"Apparently so. We will have to marry as soon as possible."

"*What?*" He had just taken going "too fast" to "light speed."

"My brother." Dominick paused as Starlight picked his way over a gully that cut across the trail. "If he finds out what happened, he will come to get you."

Janelle's head ached. "Let me see if I have this straight. If you and I marry, you become emperor and he dies. If I marry him, he stays emperor and *you* die. If either of you kills me, he dies."

"That sums it up, yes."

"If no one marries me, do things stay as they are now?"

"I think so."

"The answer is simple, then. I go home."

"And after that?" he asked. "My men know about you. So will the monks who check your hair. If you are who I believe, how long before Max finds out? If you go home, he might find you someday. I did." Then he added, "That assumes you can go back."

She suppressed a shudder. "I have to believe it's possible."

"I understand. But as long you are here, I will risk neither my life nor yours."

Janelle wondered why she couldn't have normal problems, like fixing the plumbing or finding a job. "If we marry, won't your brother die?"

"I don't want his death."

"But you want his title."

"I would be a better emperor."

"Why?"

"Maximillian is brutal man."

"What makes you any different?"

He gave a terse laugh. "I can think of no one else who would dare ask me such a thing."

Well, tough. "It's a fair question. You two are brothers."

"Your questions are too personal."

She let out an exasperated breath. "You say we have to marry so you stay alive and I don't get brutalized. That's pretty personal."

Silence.

Janelle bit back her impatience. She knew too little about Dominick to judge when to push and when to bide her time. But push she would when she had a better sense of her situation, whatever it took to find her way home.

They rode for a while with only the thud of hooves on the trail to break the silence. Eventually Dominick said, "My father raised my brother. He ignored me because I wasn't his heir. I spent my childhood with my mother. I had her love. Maximillian had whippings." His muscles corded as his hold around her tightened. "Father intended to 'shape' Max into a man like himself. He succeeded. Max is exactly like him." Anger honed his voice. "My mother is dead. I couldn't protect her. But I won't let my brother do the same to you."

His words had so many painful implications, she hardly knew how to respond. All she could say was, "I'm sorry."

He clenched the reins until his knuckles whitened. "Max and I were close as boys. He has hardened over the years. I mourn the loss of the brother I loved, but I hate what he has become."

"It must be difficult for you both."

"You are generous, to offer sympathy to those who put you in this situation."

She had no answer for that.

"Janelle." He spoke thoughtfully. "Make a bargain with me."

"How do you mean?" she asked, wary.

"Marry me, and I will do what I can to help you return home. If you get back, who is to say the marriage exists in that universe? You can resume your life without me."

Given her lack of options, he could have demanded she do what he wanted. It mattered that he asked her consent and offered his help. But she knew too little about him. So far he had acted with honor, and a kindness incongruous with his obvious capacity for violence, but she had no guarantee that would continue. Nor did she doubt his offer came with strings; he wasn't talking about a marriage in name only. Her face heated. She needed to know him better. To trust him.

"I'm not ready," she said.

"We don't have the luxury of time. This is the best way I know to protect us both."

What to do? Given how little she knew about life here, going it alone didn't seem particularly bright.

"Very well," she said. "I accept your bargain."

4

PALACE OF ARCHES

It wasn't until Dominick eased his hold that Janelle she realized how much he had tensed. He said only, "Good," which relieved her. She wasn't ready for any heart-to-heart talks with this fiancé she had just acquired.

They rode higher into the mountains, and the fog thinned until they were traveling under a sky brilliant with stars, far more than she saw in Massachusetts where she lived. The day's warmth had fled. When Janelle shivered, Dominick reached to the bags he had slung over the flanks of his biaquine. Cloth rustled, and then he folded a sheepskin around her shoulders, its fleecy side against her skin.

"Thank you," she murmured.

As they continued on, Janelle mulled over his words. She couldn't fathom why she would figure in anyone's "prophecy." Her only talents were writing proofs and solving equations. Hah. Maybe she could subdue the nefarious Maximillian with Bessel functions.

Up ahead, peaks rose out of the fog, dark against the sky. Then she realized it was a cascade of onion-bulb towers, each topped by a spire. Dominick's party approached a cliff that stood about ten feet high—no, not a cliff, but a great wall that curved away in either direction, topped by crenellations.

Eerie whistles broke the night's quiet as the biaquines gathered before the wall, stamping and snorting. A gate swung outward, huge and dark, groaning. Torchlight flickered beyond, where men were cranking giant wheels wound with rope as thick their burly arms. Courtyards lay past the gate, and beyond them stood a huge building surrounded by smaller structures. The layout resembled a European castle, but the architecture evoked the palaces of Moorish Andalusia that Janelle had visited when her family lived in Spain. Icy moonlight edged it all, turning the spires, domes, and delicate arches into frozen lace.

As much as the scene enthralled Janelle, it also bewildered her. Who had settled this land? Dominick's men spoke a dialect of English, but their names sounded Mediterranean, Arabic, or Near Eastern, with English more rarely in the mix. That described their appearance, too. Maybe the Ottoman Empire had spread farther across Europe in this universe. If East and West had blended more, the mix of colonists who settled the New World here could have been different than in her world.

They rode to a courtyard in front of the palace. An immense horseshoe arch framed the entrance of the building like the keyhole for a giant antique key. Its sides rose in pillars, and at the top, an onion-shaped arch curved out and back around to a point. Mosaics tiled the pillars and glistened like silver in the moonlight.

As their party dismounted, stable-hands swirled around them. The biaquines were taller than most horses, but Dominick swung off with little effort. He reached up, offering his arms to Janelle, his harsh features blurred by moonlight and the mist in the air. She pulled her leg over and slid down, acutely aware of how she ached everywhere. He eased her to the ground, his hold solid after the swaying gait of the biaquine.

The sheepskin had fallen off her shoulders. When she shivered. Dominick pulled her close, under a jacket he had donned earlier. It was fur-lined, not as warm as the skin, but soft and thick against her arms. For a moment, she gave in to her fatigue and buried her face against his shirt as if that would hide her from his world.

When she looked up again, Dominick brushed her hair back from her face, and calluses on his palm scraped her cheek. She wondered how he had developed them—and then remembered the swords his men wore.

"Welcome to my home," he said softly. Then he bent his head.

Janelle knew what he intended, but she froze anyway. When he kissed her, his lips felt as full as they looked, a sensual contrast to his harsh power. Before she could respond, either to push him away or to return the kiss, someone behind them coughed.

Dominick raised his head, letting go of her, and she glanced past him, relieved by the interruption. A lanky man was coming down the steps of the palace, his attempt not to stare at her all the more obvious for its lack of success. He came over and spoke with Dominick. Although Janelle couldn't catch all of their words, it sounded as if the man was reporting another raid. Dominick and his men had apparently been out searching for the outlaws, intent on stopping the harassment of his people.

Dominick turned to Janelle. "I will see you later." He took off his jacket and wrapped it around her shoulders. With a crooked smile, he added, "It looks much better on you than on me."

"Thank you," she said, uncertain how to act with him.

He climbed the steps with the other man, leaving her with two guards. She noted how easily Dominick assumed authority. He listened carefully and asked questions. When he gave orders, he did it with confidence and tact. She had seen those same qualities in the strongest leaders she had met while her father was the American Ambassador to Spain.

Bracketed by guards, she went up the steps, through a foyer, and into a hall gleaming in the light of the torches carried by Dominick's men. Janelle's breath caught. Soaring arches filled the immense hall, row after row of them, a forest of pillars in perfect lines. Tessellated mosaics in gold, blue, and green curved around columns and patterned the vaulted ceiling. In each V-shape where the arches met, a stained-glass window glowed with gem colors, showing scenes similar to those of Catholic churches in Spain. It was like an exquisite blending of Moorish art with the styles of a European cathedral, reminding her of the Cathedral-Mosque of Cordoba in Spain.

A group of men met Dominick just inside the entrance, and Janelle's guards drew her to a stop. She waited, too tired to deal with her confusion. It had to be past two in the morning.

People came and went. It wasn't long before three women appeared, walking through the arches from deeper within the palace. Silk wrapped them from neck to ankle, glistening in the smoky torchlight, crimson and saffron, shot through with gold threads. Their shimmering black hair fell to their waists.

The trio stopped in front of Janelle. The oldest woman, a matron with silver hair, spoke in melodic phrases that almost sounded like English, but that went by too fast to catch.

"I'm sorry." Janelle's voice rasped with fatigue. "I don't understand."

The woman spoke more slowly. "Come with us." She didn't smile. "To someplace you can wash. And sleep."

Relief washed over Janelle. "Thank you."

The woman just barely inclined her head, stiff and cool.

As Janelle set off with them, accompanied by her guards, she glanced back at Dominick. He remained deep in conversation with his men, and she wasn't certain he even knew she had left.

The older woman spoke curtly. "His Highness has important matters to attend."

Janelle just nodded, submerged in her fatigue. They went down a "corridor" of arches, one of many in the hall, walkways delineated by columns instead of walls. It was dizzying, all that geometrical beauty gleaming in the torchlight.

The older woman was watching her face. "This hall is why Prince Dominick-Michael's home is called the Palaces of Arches."

"It's glorious," Janelle said. "Is this the Hall of Arches?"

"No. The Fourier Hall."

"Fourier?" Janelle blinked. "Like the mathematician?"

The woman gave a sharp wave of her hand. "It has always been called this. That is all I know."

Janelle didn't push. Having lived as the child of a diplomat for so many years had taught her a great deal about dealing with cultures other than her own, and she could tell her interactions here were on shaky ground. She had discovered early on that if she wasn't certain how her words would be received, it was better to say nothing.

She couldn't stop staring at the arches, though. What an exquisite challenge it would be to portray those graceful repeating patterns as a periodic function.

Their Fourier transform would be a work of art. An unsteady urge to laugh hit her, followed by the desire to sit down and put her head in her hands. Such a strange thought, that she could capture in mathematics the essence of a dream palace that couldn't exist.

The women's slippered feet padded on the tiled floor, and Janelle's running shoes squeaked. At the back of the hall, they passed under a huge arch built from gold-veined marble rather than the wood in the Fourier Hall. A true corridor lay beyond, with stone walls tiled in star mosaics. Its size dwarfed their party, and other halls intersected it at oddly sharp angles. Pillars stood at corners where the halls met, each carved to portray a man with a great broad sword or a woman in elegantly draped robes holding a long-stemmed flower. It spoke to the European influence here that the designs included human statues, which didn't appear in Moorish architecture.

Janelle tried to keep track of their route through the maze of halls, but exhaustion dulled her mind. She was lost by the time they stopped at an oaken door. The guards stayed outside while the women took her into a small room. Plush rugs covered the floor, and mosaics with pink tulips and swirling green stems graced the lower half of the walls. Something odd about the stems tugged at her mind, but she was too tired to puzzle it out. A white table stood on one corner supporting a blue vase with real flowers. Blue velvet bedcovers lay in another corner, on a thicker pile of rugs, with pillows heaped there like a tumble of rose and jade clouds.

"It's beautiful," Janelle said. "Thank you."

No one answered. They led her across the room and under an archway. In the chamber beyond, a small, sunken pool steamed and a lamp glowed in a sea-shell claw on the wall.

The older woman finally spoke. "We can help you bathe."

Janelle's face heated. "It's kind of you to offer. But I can manage."

"Then we will leave you to rest." The woman was so aloof, she could have been a hundred miles away. The trio bowed gracefully and exited the chamber. A moment later, the outer door creaked on its hinges.

Janelle hoped she hadn't just committed some social blunder. Unsure what she would find, she returned to the bedroom. An oil lamp hung on a scrolled hook by the entrance. It gave less light than the torches, but she preferred the lamp, which neither smoked nor sputtered. To her relief, the door had a lock on this side, which meant she could keep people from entering, assuming they didn't have a key.

The door opened when she tried it. One of her guards stood a short distance down the hall, severe in his leather armor. Light from a wall sconce glinted on the hilt of the broadsword strapped across on his back.

"Hello," Janelle said.

He turned with a start. Then he said what sounded like, "My greetings, Lady."

"Isn't that sword heavy?" she asked.

He seemed bemused by her attention. "Not for me."

"Oh. Good." She wasn't sure why she asked, but she felt the need to connect to people, to make this less strange. "Goodnight."

His craggy face softened. "Goodnight."

Janelle closed the door and sagged against the wall. She could think of many reasons Dominick might post a guard: to keep her in, as a courtesy, or because she wasn't safe even in his home. For all its extraordinary beauty, his world had a starkness that kept her off balance.

Ill-at-ease, she explored her suite. In the bathing room, an elegantly carved bench stood against one wall, set with a jade-green towel, a silver brush inlaid with mother-of-pearl disks, two soaps carved like tulips, and a crimson silk robe. It was all gorgeous, everything handmade. The suite, however, had only that one exit with the guard. They had closed her in well.

No one said you couldn't leave, she told herself. Besides, more than anything else right now, she just wanted to clean up. She carried the soaps to the pool, an oval filled with scented water, but then she hesitated. The idea of undressing made her feel vulnerable. The grimy scrapes on her arms and legs decided her; she quickly peeled off her clothes, shivering as the cold air chilled her bare skin. Then she slid into the heated pool.

Warmth seeped blissfully into her body as she lay back. Silence filled the room, a contrast to the muted city roar she had lived with these last years at MIT. No sirens or engines interrupted the quiet, none of the constant hum that rumbled even in the deepest hours of an urban night. She was immersed in a great ocean of quietude.

Her thoughts drifted to Dominick's gate. A branch cut? In mathematics, they came from complex numbers. She could write such a number as Z, where

$$Z = \exp(i\theta).$$

The term θ was called the phase angle. Varying the phase from $\theta=0$ to $\theta=2\pi$ was like going around an analog clock from 12 to 12. Just as 12 was the same at the start and finish, so 0 and 2π were the same. However, if she divided θ by 2, then

$$Z = \exp(i\theta/2).$$

Now the phase was $\theta/2$. As θ went from 0 to 2π, the phase only changed to π. The angle θ had to go around a second time before $\theta/2$ returned to its starting value of 2π. But the same θ couldn't have two different values of Z. To avoid that contradiction, Z slipped through a branch cut and went onto a second sheet for the second cycle θ. Just as 3 am and 3 pm were different times, so θ on each sheet was considered different. Her world was one "clock" and Dominick's was another.

That suggested some phase here had to go through a full cycle before Dominick's gate reopened. But the phase of what? Her twelve-hour model was only an analogy; she had no idea how long would she have to wait before the actual gate reopened. Days? Months? Years?

Nor was that her only problem. Suppose she divided θ by 3. The phase would be θ/3. It meant she would need three "clocks." Three universes. Divide θ by 4, and she needed four. Who knew how many sheets could exist? For all she knew, if she went through a gate, she could end up on yet some other clock—some other universe—instead of her own.

Janelle groaned. Her head hurt and the water had cooled. Putting away her thoughts, she soaped her body and washed her hair. Then she climbed out and dried off with the luxuriant towel. She reached for her wrinkled sundress, then paused. The robe was far nicer and scented with perfume, certainly more pleasant than her gritty clothes. She slipped on the robe, and the sensuous glide of silk against her bare skin stirred her thoughts of Dominick. She tried to smile at her reflection in the pool. "Hey, Aulair, you look hot." But her voice shook like the ripples in over the water.

She padded barefoot into the other room. She was so tired she could barely stand, but she felt too exposed to sleep. The bed consisted of no more than layers of rugs covered by a velvet comforter. She sat on it in one corner with the wall at her back, facing the door as she drew the pillows around her. It wasn't until they crumpled in her grip that she realized how hard she was clenching them.

Her eyelids drooped and she forced them up. She wouldn't sleep. The lamp swung on its hook, moving shadows on the walls, back and forth, back and forth . . .

The scrape of wood against stone roused Janelle. She lifted her head, disoriented. She had slid down and was lying amid the pillows. The lamp had burned low, leaving the room swathed in shadows.

The scrape came again. She thought she said, *Who is it?* but no words came out.

The door swung slowly inward. Dominick stood in the archway, filling it with his height and his presence. The dim light turned his shirt a darker blue and glinted on the hilt of his sheathed dagger. The way he loomed, his face harsh and starkly intense, evoked the specter of conquerors who swept across continents, laying waste to their enemies.

Janelle pulled herself up so she was half lying, half sitting, reclined in the pillows. "Hello." She barely managed the word. Such a quiet greeting for so dramatic a man.

"May I come in?" His voice rumbled.

She appreciated that he asked, given that he could do whatever he wanted. "Yes," she said.

He entered and the room seemed to shrink. After closing the door, he came over and knelt on the other side of the bed. His shirt was open at the neck, revealing a tuft of chest hair, black and curly.

"Have you slept?" he asked.

"A little." She wondered how the rest of his chest looked.

He watched her watching him and his lips curved upward. The shadows eased the hard edges of his face. Sitting on the bed, he tugged off one of his boots.

Whoa. Now he was taking off the other boot. He set it next to the first and started to undo his shirt.

"Wait." Her cheeks flamed. If she hadn't been so groggy, she would have realized sooner what she was agreeing to when she invited him into her room.

Dominick paused. "No?"

"I can't. I mean—that is—"

He waited. Then he asked, "Do you want me to leave?"

"I don't want to be alone. But I don't—" She stuttered to a halt, feeling like an idiot.

"It's all right." He slid across the rugs and stretched out on his side facing her, with his head propped up on one hand. He took up the entire length of the bed. She could see why he liked sleeping on the floor; his legs were too long for a mattress.

"My monks checked your hair," he said. "You are Janelle Aulair."

"Oh, well, I knew that." She was practically stuttering.

He trailed his finger along her hip, sliding up the robe, which suddenly seemed too short. "This is pretty."

She put his hand back on the bedspread. Maybe she should ask him to leave. But she didn't want to be alone. He continued to watch her, his head tilted to the side as if she were a puzzle.

"You must have more names than Dominick," she said.

"Indeed I do. Dominick-Michael Alexander Constantine."

Now *that* was a moniker. "Those names are famous in my universe." She was talking too fast again. "Like Alexander the Great."

"The Great." His gaze turned sleepy, as if he were a satisfied cat. "Tell me more."

"He conquered Persia—" She stopped as he tugged the sash of her robe. His knuckles brushed her inner thigh.

"Don't," Janelle said.

He traced his finger along her cheek. "Do I offend you so much?"

"Sweet heaven, no."

"Good." His voice was like whiskey, dark and potent. "Otherwise, this would be a rather uneventful wedding night."

She flushed. "You have the wedding night before the wedding?"

"If the bride and groom agree, yes."

"What if they don't agree?"

"I thought you did."

There was that. "If you stay tonight, are we, uh, married?"

He watched her face. "If that is the agreement reached and the bride receives rings from the groom, then yes. But the public ceremonies are traditional and expected, especially for the royal family."

"Oh." She hesitated. "Does that happen tomorrow?"

"In the morning."

"It's just all so strange."

"For me, also." He stroked his knuckles along her thigh. "But not unwelcome."

"Dominick . . ."

He rubbed the hem of her robe between his thumb and finger. "This cloth is beautiful on you." He slid up to her, then put his finger under her chin and tilted up her face. He kissed her deeply and she tensed, both wanting him to stop and wanting him to keep going. Her only experience with seduction was on the level of sending out for pizza and Cokes; she was so far out of her depth here, she was drowning. But oh, what a way to go.

He pulled her closer and eased the robe off her shoulders. As he slid his palm over her breast, his calluses scraped her nipple, and she felt good in places where he wasn't touching her. Then he drew back, his face unexpectedly tender.

"Women are so small," he said. "Look at this." He put the heel of his hand at the bottom of her rib cage. His palm stretched up her torso and his fingers closed around her breast. "I can hold so much of you, but you couldn't even cover my ribs."

His ribs. Clever, sexy man. Of course she looked at his chest where he had unfastened his shirt. A mat of hair curled over his muscles. She laid her palm against his abdomen, feeling the springy hair, the hard muscles. Very nice. Very intimidating.

"You smell like flowers," he said. Laying her on her back, he stretched out on top of her, easing his hips between her thighs. Then he reached for the waistband of his trousers.

"Wait!" Janelle face burned. He didn't seem to have any speed between *pause* and *fast forward*.

Dominick lifted his head, his eyes glossy with arousal. "Wait?"

"No more." She felt like a fool, but she had just discovered she couldn't do this with someone she barely knew, even if he would be her husband tomorrow.

He brushed his lips across hers. "I won't hurt you."

"Dominick, I—no. No more."

Frustration crept into his voice. "You tease me."

"I don't mean to. I just—I can't."

"First your behavior says yes. Then no. Then yes. Then no. Which is it?"

"I'm not ready."

He lay there, propped up on his hands, and she knew they both realized the truth. He could do whatever he wanted and she couldn't stop him. She lay still, meeting his gaze.

Dominick groaned and rolled off her, onto his back. Then he threw his arm over his eyes and inhaled deeply. He stayed there, completely still except for the rise and fall of his chest.

Gradually his breathing slowed. Finally he lowered his arm and turned his head to her. "You are an unusual woman."

Well, that was certainly tactful. A lot better than *Make up your damn mind.* She wanted to hold him, to feel safe, but she wasn't safe with him. Although she didn't think he meant to force her, he would get angry if he thought she was deliberately leading him on, and she could end up with more than she bargained for. She could also, she realized, end up pregnant.

Dominick studied her with that close focus of his. "I don't mean to pressure you." He smiled ruefully. "But you are so lovely, Janelle. Difficult to resist."

Her face heated. "You do sweet-talk a girl." The southern drawl she had lost after her family moved to Washington D. C. often slipped back into her voice when she was nervous.

"It may be 'sweet-talk.' But I mean what I say." He took off only his shirt, nothing more. Then he slid down the velvet cover and drew it over them both. Settling on his back, he pulled her into his arms. She closed her eyes, relieved, letting her head rest in the hollow where his arm met his shoulder.

"Dream well," he murmured.

"You too."

Dominick soon fell asleep, his eyes twitching under his lids. As she drifted into slumber, she wondered if he dreamed of the towns and countryside that would someday fall to his army. He could be gentle with her, but she had no doubt he was capable of conquering a continent.

Would he ravage his world with the ambition that led men to create empires—at immense human cost?

5

THE SHATTERED HALL

Birdsong awoke Janelle. She lay in a pleasant haze, listening to the dawn.

Then she remembered.

Her eyes snapped open. It was real. She was still in the palace. Early morning light filtered through high window slits she hadn't seen last night. The room otherwise looked as she remembered, beautiful and spare. And empty. Dominick had gone.

She rubbed her eyes. Yesterday she had been a new graduate with good prospects; today she had nothing but the unknown. She thought of Rupert Quarterstaff, the lawyer who dealt with her inheritance. Two years ago, when she had been paralyzed by grief, Rupert had stepped her through the estate settlement with a solicitude that went beyond his professional duties. He expected to see her in a few days. What would he do when she didn't show? It would be a mess.

Janelle sat up, rubbing her eyes. She couldn't stay here as the plaything of a warlord who wanted to conquer half of North America. She needed a library. *Someone* had invented Dominick's gate. She had to figure out how and why.

Pushing off the covers, she shivered in the cold air. She went into the other room and bathed, then dried off with a towel someone had left while she slept. Her clothes from yesterday were gone. As she searched for something to wear, she kept noticing the walls. Something strange, what. . . ?

Stepping closer, she peered at the mosaics. Wavelike curves were intertwined in the tulip designs. She hadn't seen them clearly last night because they were the same color as the swirling stems. The curves weren't just wavelike, they *were* waves, sinusoids, harmonics, quantum wave functions, beautiful and elegant. They were too accurate for coincidence; someone had understood them well enough to reproduce the curves. It was another piece of this whacked-out puzzle, along with the Fourier Hall and Riemann gate.

Deep in thought, she returned to the bedroom. Someone had come in while she bathed; her robe was gone and the bed had been remade with fresh rugs and a jade-green bedspread. As she toweled her hair, she surveyed the empty room. She couldn't dress without clothes.

When the doorknob turned, she jumped. She barely had time to wrap herself in the towel before the door opened. The three women from last night stood there, each holding a large box decorated with abalone and opals.

"Uh . . . good morning." Janelle kept the towel clutched around her body.

Her greeting seemed to be the signal they expected. They bowed and entered the room. The older woman took an ornate key off a hook under the lamp and handed it to a soldier outside. After he closed the door, a loud click came from the lock.

Janelle watched them uneasily. "Why did he lock us in?"

"For privacy." The older woman spoke in the same slow voice she had used last night. "I am Farimah." She introduced the younger women as Silvia and Danae.

Janelle understood their dialect a little better this morning. It reminded her of the times she had spent with the families of dignitaries who visited her father, how she had striven to learn their language. For her, new words had always been like gems strung together to create bright necklaces of meaning.

"What can I do for you?" she asked. Her towel slipped down her breast and she flushed as she pulled it back up.

Danae offered her box. "It's for your wedding."

"Oh." Janelle cleared her throat. "Right. Yes."

"The ceremony will take place immediately," Farimah said. "His Highness has had word that the Emperor's army gathers in the south. Prince Dominick-Michael and his men must leave today to discover what Maximillian plans."

Well, that was romantic; her groom intended to spend his honeymoon spying on his brother. It would give her time to adjust, though, and to learn about the gate.

"We can wait for the ceremony until he returns," Janelle offered.

Farimah's voice took on even more of an edge. "He wishes otherwise."

"Here, Lady Janelle." Danae spoke in a sweeter voice, opening her box to reveal a treasure, gold hoops and rings, all inset with mother-of-pearl.

"They're stunning," Janelle said. "But goodness, I can't accept that."

Farimah stiffened. "Generations of Constantine brides have worn these with pride. You consider yourself above them?"

"No. No, I didn't mean that." Mortified, she tried again. "I just don't want to presume."

Farimah gave her a look that plainly translated into *You do.* But she only said, "His Highness wishes you to have them."

"It's kind of Dominick," Janelle said.

Farimah jerked up her hand as if to strike her. Then she took a deep breath and lowered her arm. Her voice was ice. "You will refer to His Highness as Prince Dominick-Michael."

Janelle wondered if she could say anything right. "I'm sorry. He told me to call him Dominick."

"Ai," Silvia murmured. She glanced at Farimah with sympathy. To Janelle, she said, "Farimah did not know."

Before Janelle could further cram her foot down her throat and tickle her tonsils with her toes, Danae intervened by coming over and fastening a luminous torque around Janelle's neck.

"These jewels will help ensure your safety," Danae told her.

Janelle squinted at her. "My safety from what?"

Silvia clipped a bracelet around Janelle's wrist. "The heirlooms indicate you are wife to the emperor's brother. With so much unrest in the provinces, a woman needs more protection than in normal times."

Well, that sounded just dandy. Running her fingers over the necklace, she realized it was a delicate version of the heavy chain Dominick wore. The bracelet had the same pattern as the abalone in his shirt cuffs.

While Farimah put a belled chain around each of Janelle's ankles, Silvia took out a blue velvet cloth with gold highlights. Then she waited. Janelle blinked at her.

Farimah sighed as she rose to her feet. "It would be easier to dress you without the towel."

"Oh." Her face burning, Janelle let the cloth drop to the floor.

"Goodness," Silvia said, as if Janelle had achieved an impressive feat instead of just standing there naked and feeling like an idiot.

"No wonder he wants to marry you so fast," Farimah muttered. "Men see only one thing."

Silvia put the velvet cloth around Janelle's hips. The skirt fit low on her pelvis, showing too much of her abdomen. The hem almost reached her knees, but a slit went up the left side to her hip.

Janelle flushed. "I can't wear this."

"Why?" Farimah asked. "It appears to fit."

"It shows too much skin."

Danae laughed good-naturedly. "What is a wedding for, but to entice the groom?"

"Come now," Farimah said. She knelt by her box and withdrew a girdle designed from beaten coins with a border of little gold bells. Janelle stood awkwardly while they fastened it around her hips. Heavy and snug, the girdle fit over the skirt and sparkled with sapphires and mother-of-pearl. It jangled when she moved. Then Silvia brought out a bra made from silver coins, with loops of abalone and opal beads.

For flaming sake. "I *can't* wear that," Janelle stated. Enough was enough.

Silvia considered the halter and then Janelle. "You are right. It is too small."

"I didn't mean my breasts," Janelle said. No one listened. Silvia went to the door and knocked.

The guard outside only opened the door just a bit, and Silvia blocked his view of the room. But a child squeezed past her anyway, a girl of about three with black curls and a sweet face. Silvia glanced back at Janelle, her gaze malicious, then slipped outside and closed the door. As Janelle stiffened, wondering what she had done to evoke Silvia's hostility, the child ran to Farimah.

"Fami!" the little girl cried, reaching out her arms.

Farimah's face underwent an amazing transformation, becoming warm and affectionate as she laughed and reached for the child. But in mid-motion, Farimah suddenly froze, her gaze flashing to Janelle. Panic surged over her face.

Puzzled, Janelle gave the child a friendly smile. "Hello."

The girl backed up and hid her face in Farimah's skirts.

Farimah lifted the child into her arms, her attention riveted on Janelle. "My apology." She sounded terrified. "I didn't realize she had followed me here."

"It's all right," Janelle said. Both Farimah and Danae had gone deathly pale. *Why?* "She is welcome to stay."

"Thank you." Farimah spoke with stiff formality.

"She's charming," Janelle said. "What's her name?"

"Selena. Like her mother."

"You seem to know her well."

"She is my granddaughter." Farimah took a breath. "I also care for her siblings. Her mother died in childbirth."

"I'm sorry," Janelle murmured.

The girl was watching her with big dark eyes that somehow looked familiar. "You Mama now?" she asked.

Mama? *Mama?* Ah, hell. Janelle stared at Farimah. "She is Dominick's child?"

Farimah met her gaze. "Yes."

Life was growing messier by the moment. "How many does he have?"

"Five." Farimah was as taut as a coil. "The oldest is twelve."

Janelle wondered just when her new groom had planned to mention he had a family. "Are they all your daughter's children?"

"Of course!" An angry red flush appeared in her cheeks. "After Selena came into his life, His Highness had no other women."

Janelle rubbed her neck, trying to ease her aching muscles. Selena hardly sounded like a concubine, if Dominick had lived monogamously with her for so many years. Had some stupid prophecy kept them from marrying? No wonder Farimah seemed like she wanted to toss Janelle off the mountain.

Farimah's fear also made sense now. Janelle spoke quietly. "Your grandchildren are welcome in my household."

The older woman just nodded, her posture rigid. But her frozen look thawed a bit. She took the girl to the door and gave her into the keeping of someone outside.

Silvia returned then, watching them with an avid gaze. Janelle wanted to sock her. Silvia could have kept the girl outside and protected Farimah from that heart-stopping moment when the grandmother realized *she* would have to tell Janelle about the children. What had Silvia hoped to achieve? It didn't take a genius to see women had little power here. It created a dynamic foreign to Janelle, an unstated enmity and maneuvering for sexual power. Silvia was a beauty, with glossy black hair and a voluptuous figure. Had she hoped for

Dominick's favor? Maybe she believed discord between his new wife and the mother of his former favorite could work to her advantage.

Janelle had no interest in such machinations. Compared to this place, her world was so enlightened it glowed in the dark. She didn't think women here would be burning their bras any time soon. Given the halter Silvia was holding, they would have to melt the damn things.

At least this one fit better than the last, though "fit" was a generous description. It held her breasts in a scanty gold mesh with a few jewels in strategic places and more of those bells fringing the bottom. Her groom would certainly have no trouble finding her, given all the noise she would make in this outfit.

"This is the most appallingly prehistoric contraption I have ever seen," Janelle muttered.

Her companions regarded her politely. Frustrated, she added, "Why are there guards outside of my door?"

"As far as we know," Danae said carefully, "Emperor Maximillian has no idea you are here."

"And if he did?" Janelle asked.

"I would never speak ill of the emperor," Farimah said, "to suggest he might brutalize you out of spite for Prince Dominick-Michael."

Janelle felt queasier by the moment. "Are all women here treated this way?"

"Those with value are protected," Silvia told her.

Janelle squinted at her. "I'm afraid to ask what 'value' means."

"I should think it is obvious," Farimah said. "Beauty. Youth. Fertility. Good birth. Gentle nature. Intelligence. You obviously have the first two. Maybe a few of the others." She shrugged. "So if you lack the last, it does not matter."

Ouch. Janelle barely held back her retort. But she said only, "I really don't need to wear all these presents. Just my dress from before is fine."

"Of course," Danae murmured as if she were soothing a spooked horse. Or biaquine. Or whatever spooked here besides MIT graduates. No one made any move to bring her sun dress.

They inflicted make-up on her next. Silvia brushed her hair, working until she had dried and fluffed up the curls. Then they took her into the bathing chamber, where a long mirror hung on the wall. Her reflection stopped her cold. She glistened in gold and sea colors. Her eyes looked larger and bluer than normal, and her hair floated around her shoulders like a gold cloud. Even her bangs curled in traitorous perfection. She had to admit, the effect was impressive, and in that it became seductive. They turned her into a woman of mystery and beauty, and it tempted her to believe it increased her worth. That wasn't a path she wanted to go down, one where her intelligence and character had less value than her body or fleeting youth.

"That isn't me," Janelle said.

"It will please Prince Dominick-Michael," Silvia answered with strained patience. "That is the purpose, is it not?"

"What about pleasing his bride?" Janelle asked.

Farimah threw up her hands. "You are *marrying* him."

"Only because of a prophecy."

"Yes." Farimah's voice quieted. "Because of the prophesy."

They left her then, so she could "prepare" for the ceremony. She had no clue what that entailed, but she suspected she was supposed to think of ways to entice the groom. Hah. She should entertain herself by deriving equations for the sinusoids on the walls. That ought to stir up Dominick's libido.

Well, she had to do *something*. She stepped up on the bench in the bathroom and looked out the window—at a spectacular panorama. Mountains towered on both sides, east and west. In the south, before her, they dropped to a mesa several miles distant, where mounted riders moved in chess-like patterns. Dominick's army? It had thousands of men. She hoped that qualified as a large military, one comparable to the emperor's, if Dominick's brother was as bad as everyone implied. Then again, maybe Maximillian was a saint and Dominick just coveted his throne, as disenfranchised brothers had since time immemorial.

Wood grated against stone in the other room. Janelle jerked around, startled. That sounded like the door. She jumped off the bench and returned to the bedroom to find a group of strangers waiting for her. Six older women stood in the front, their carriage and jewels surely marking them as noblewomen. Blue silk wraps covered them from neck to ankle, making Janelle even more self-conscious about her skimpy attire. Behind them, an array of servants carried platters of food.

They offered her the feast and waited while she ate. Everyone declined to join, but no one seemed offended by her invitation to share the food. The meal was delicious. Odd, with Janelle standing up, surrounded by silent people, sampling foods and wine. Strong wine. Well, good. Right now, a few shots of whiskey would have done nicely.

When she finished, they took her outside. Twelve warriors waited in the corridor, hulking in armor, with what looked like ceremonial broadswords strapped across their backs, the gilded hilts inlaid with jewels. While the servants took off, carrying the platters with them, the noblewomen and soldiers escorted Janelle the other way, down a windowless hall lit by oil lamps in gilded scones on the walls. She went in a daze. She wanted to believe this was a delirium; a car had hit her and she was lying in a hospital. But it felt too real.

Up ahead, shouts echoed in the halls. Apparently the castle populace was excited about the wedding. Their reaction seemed out of place with the reserve of the people here. Apparently she wasn't the only one who thought so; her escorts were slowing down, their foreheads creased with puzzlement. It turned out the broadswords they wore weren't ceremonial after all, for the men were drawing the weapons. The honed blades glittered in the wavering lamplight.

Crashes sounded in the distance. More shouts came, and the halls vibrated

with a great pounding. The guards split their group into two, half of the warriors taking the noblewomen one way and the others hurrying Janelle into a side
corridor. Her escorts ran with drilled precision, taking her with them, while all
around them the rumble intensified.

A rangy soldier kept pace with Janelle. "We will go to tunnels under the palace," he said, slow enough for her to understand even though they were running.
"They exit into the mountains."

She nodded, rationing her breath.

The rumble surged into a roar—and raiders thundered out of a cross-hall,
all astride biaquines. The man in front brought his mount to an abrupt halt
and it reared, its hooves smashing the pillar of an arch that framed the corridor. Dominick's men skidded to a stop, but momentum carried the groups
together. Biaquine screams rent the air and metal rang as swords flashed. Janelle
had about as much military knowledge as a toadstool, but it took no expert to
see Dominick's men were outnumbered and in trouble. She couldn't understand
how the outlaws had broken into such a well-defended fortress.

The rangy soldier from Dominick's men pulled Janelle into a side hall, and
they sprinted down the corridor. The bells on her damn clothes chimed as if
announcing their location. Only a few lamps lit the area, but despite the dim
light, her guard took the turns with confidence, always choosing hallways too
narrow for a biaquine to follow them.

Until they hit a dead end.

"Ah, no!" Janelle stopped, heaving in air. They were *trapped*.

"Don't worry." The guard stepped into a wall recess and pushed the tiles in
what looked like a combination.

"What happened back there?" she asked.

He glanced at her, his craggy face drawn. "I cannot say. I saw no symbols
I recognized on those men." He leaned into the wall and it slid inward, revealing a tunnel. Straightening up, he took a lamp off a hook in the recess and then
motioned Janelle forward.

She entered the passage. "Do you think they came to stop the wedding?"

"I doubt it." He shut the door, closing out the distant clamor. As they headed
along the path, he spoke in a quieter voice. "Emperor Maximillian is the person with the most reason to stop it, and those weren't his men. Nor would he
raid his brother's home. Even if he were willing to commit such an atrocity, too
much chance exists that in the heat of the attack, you would be killed despite his
orders. He wouldn't risk it."

Janelle blanched. His answer had an obvious corollary: whoever *was* raiding
the palace had no qualms about killing her or anyone else.

They followed an ancient tunnel. Cracks cut through the walls and lichen
encrusted them in eerie patterns. It wouldn't have surprised her to see a wraith
coalesce in the recesses where shadows pooled. The damp air smelled musty
and the stone chilled her bare feet. She shivered, wishing she had more clothes.

Then it hit Janelle: not all those marks on the walls were cracks. Wave functions oscillated down here, too, engraved in the stone.

She indicated the patterns. "What are those designs for?"

"Artwork," her guard answered. "They're all over the palace." He looked apologetic. "These tunnels aren't kept up well. The levels above are in better repair."

"Ah. I see." In truth, she didn't see at all. The designs looked ancient, which made no sense.

A murmur of flowing water came from ahead. The path widened into an open area where a crude rail blocked the way, with walkways curving to either side. She went to the rail and looked down into a well about ten feet across. It plunged into darkness. She toed a pebble over the edge and a good five seconds passed before she heard a faint splash.

Janelle shuddered. "I'm glad that wasn't one of us." Pushed by an invader.

The warrior spoke gruffly. "It is a cruel business, this life." He motioned to the walkway on the right. "This should take us to another set of tunnels."

They followed the path—and neither of them saw the break until almost too late. Janelle had already stepped forward when the lamplight revealed the ground had collapsed into the well. She jerked back and stumbled into the guard. Grasping her shoulder with a steadying hand, he held her until she caught her balance.

Janelle stared bleakly at the fissure. It was too large to jump, and the rail that bordered the well to the left was broken. Although two sheets of wood lay across the gap, neither looked solid. Whatever bridge they had once belonged to had fallen into neglect.

Her guard squinted at the boards. "Maybe we can go another way."

She blew out a gust of air, stirring tendrils of hair around her face. "I hope so."

They tried the left side, but the break extended through the path there as well. The tunnel contained nothing they could use to repair the bridge, and the well rail wasn't strong enough to bridge the gap.

The chill seeped into Janelle and the clink of her clothes seemed loud in the still air. She pried off the bracelets and anklets and hid them in a crack to retrieve later—if she survived to tell anyone. She couldn't remove the girdle because it held on her skirt, but at least she didn't jangle as much.

The guard knelt to examine the boards that crossed the fissure. "I think these can hold you. Perhaps me, but I can't be sure." He looked up at her. "If we go back, you might be killed. Or captured, which could be worse."

"What will happen to you?" she asked.

His gaze never wavered. "I serve Prince Dominick-Michael."

Janelle understood what he didn't say. "To get to me, they would have to kill you."

His face gentled. "Do not look so dismayed. In battle, death is always possible."

Please, God, not today. She knelt next to him. "Can we wait here?"

"I think it unwise. People know of these tunnels." He indicated the shadows beyond the break. "The passages that way will let you escape the palace. You must not be caught. The rest is secondary."

"Your life isn't secondary to me."

"I thank you. But it is my honor to serve Prince Dominick-Michael." He handed her the lamp. "You try first, in case the bridge won't hold me."

"But if you can't cross, you won't have any light."

His grin flashed. "That will make it harder for our enemies to find me, eh?"

It amazed her that he could joke at such a time. She managed a smile for him. "You're too smart for them with or without light." She took a deep breath, then stepped onto the bridge. She walked forward, her hand clenched on the lamp, and the span bent under her weight.

Halfway over, one of the boards snapped.

Janelle flailed, dropping the lamp, and it plummeted into the well. As she fell to her knees on the remaining board, darkness closed around her. A splash took away the last hint of light.

"Lady Janelle?" Her guard's voice was rough with concern.

"Here." Her voice shook. More loudly, she said, "I'm here."

"Blessed Almighty! Are you all right?"

"Almost." She inched forward on her hands and knees. "I'm not to the other side yet."

"You can make it." He sounded as if he was trying to convince himself as much as her.

From your lips to God's ear. She moved another inch and her knuckles hit the broken edges of the path. Even as relief surged over her, the remaining board creaked. In the same instant that she threw herself forward, the board broke in two and dropped out from under her. Her torso landed flat on the path, but her legs hung into the fissure. She scrabbled at the ground, frantic as rocks fragmented under her and clattered away.

With a heave, Janelle hauled herself onto the path and sprawled on her stomach. She groaned as the girdle jabbed her skin.

"Lady!" the guard called.

"I'm h-here." The pound of her heart felt like storm waves. "The boards fell. You have to stay there."

"Ah." He sounded subdued. "You must go on alone, then."

Janelle climbed to her feet and stood, swaying, dizzy. When her head cleared, she said, "Will you tell me your name?" She didn't want to leave without even knowing who had helped her, at risk to her own life.

"I am Kadar." He paused. "If I do not see you again—I would like to say—" He stopped.

"Yes?" Janelle asked.

"We have heard how you were pulled into our land," His deep voice was kind. "Given all that has happened, you could have hated us and denied our prince. Instead, you treat us with grace. I am just a soldier. I have no great knowledge of other places. But it seems to me that you are a gift to His Highness."

Good Lord. Janelle had thought she mostly offended people here. She could have done better if she hadn't been so bewildered. But she had always valued the opportunity to experience other cultures. Her parents had left her with a treasured memory of how they honored the depth and range of the world's peoples. It didn't make her willing to tolerate mistreatment; she had a temper she had to watch, and she reacted strongly when she saw injustice. But according to their ways, Dominick and his people had treated her well.

She spoke quietly. "Thank you, Kadar."

He became all business then, describing the tunnels ahead. Then he said, "The prince has a hunting lodge in the forest. The last passage will let you out near there. I'll meet you at the lodge."

She rubbed the goose bumps on her arms. "Don't you get killed."

His voice lightened. "I shall endeavor not to. Farewell for now."

"Good-bye." Janelle set off, keeping her right palm on the wall for guidance. No light softened the darkness; she couldn't even see her other hand in front of her face. She went with care, probing each step with her foot before she put down her weight. But she didn't dare take too long; she had no idea who else knew about these tunnels or would discover them.

Her palm hit stone. A dead end. Alarm surged through her, but she pushed it down and searched the surface. She did indeed find tiles, as Kadar had described, and she pushed them in the sequence he had given her. When she leaned into the wall, it slid inward with a creaking protest and swung aside. She ventured on, into more of the suffocating darkness.

It felt as if she walked for hours. Then she noticed a change; the air had warmed. A scent of pine wafted around her, a welcome change from the stench of musty stone. Even more encouraging, she could see her hand. Up ahead, light sifted through a crevice shaded by fir trees. She was free!

Voices drifted to her from outside.

Janelle stopped and swore silently. The speakers were in front of the opening. She could understand enough of their words to figure out they were sentries for the raiders. Clenching one fist, she retreated back along the tunnel.

Boots clanked at the exit.

Damn! That had to be the sentries. Keeping her slow, silent pace became excruciating; it was all she could do to break out running, which would of course start her wretched clothes jangling.

After an eon, she reached the place where she had opened the secret door. The sentries were closer. A man cussed and another laughed. She slipped past the door, then hesitated, knowing she had only two options: close the door and alert them she was here, but block them from following her; or continue on in silence and risk them finding her in the dark.

Janelle made her decision. Grabbing the edges of the door, she pulled hard. It swung closed with a screech of stone on stone, and she barely managed to snatch away her hands before it crashed into place.

A shout came from the other side, muffled by the stone. Then a heavy object slammed the door.

She stumbled forward, away from the door, with her hands raised in the dark. *Where to go?* If she retraced her steps, she would end up trapped at the fissure. Kadar had said another path led off from this junction; a true dead-end would make the secret entrance too obvious. Except she could find nothing, nothing in the dark, *nothing at all—*

Janelle stumbled into the opening with a grunt. Yes! It was here, a passage that slanted sharply to the right. She followed it, wanting to run but holding back, afraid of finding another open chasm. The darkness weighed on her, smothering and dank. She imagined specters at every step, terrors crouched low or clinging to the walls, waiting for her to dislodge them.

Wings brushed her face, and furry bodies. Janelle pressed her fist against her mouth to stop her scream. She sagged against the wall and folded her arms across her body while she shook.

Bats. It's only bats. She stretched out her arms and forced herself to go on. Distant crashes rumbled as the sentries beat at the door. No way back existed, only forward into the dark.

Suddenly her palms hit wood: another dead-end. She searched the wall, sliding her hands frantically over the rough, splintered surface. Nothing. *Nothing.*

Wait! Here was a latch, up high on the wall. She had to stand on her toes to reach it. As her fingertips scraped against the rusted metal catch, a tiny window creaked open. She peered out—and gratitude flooded over her.

The Fourier Hall lay beyond the door.

With light filtering in the window, she managed a better search and found the aged gears that locked the door. They crumbled under her touch, as did the lock. She inched the door open and slipped out into the hall. Walking softly through the forest of pillars, she headed for the palace entry. The great double doors were open, revealing an overcast day outside. Freedom.

Hooves clattered behind her.

Janelle whirled around—and barely ducked in time to evade a bare-headed rider leaning down in his saddle to grab her. His biaquine pounded past her under the tall arches.

Janelle sprinted for the entrance, and the rider came around in front of her. As he reined in his mount, it side-stepped toward her. Without pause, she spun around and fled the other way, back through the arches. Tiles shattered behind her as the man pursued on his biaquine. She swerved into another row of arches, and a splintering crack sounded, followed by an oath. Glancing back as she ran, she saw an arch collapsing around the rider as his biaquine tried to turn in too confined an area. She kept running.

More shouts rang through the air and hooves pounded the floor. Riders were pouring into the hall from deeper within the palace, thundering down the columned aisles straight toward her.

"No!" Janelle skidded to a stop. She reversed direction, but the outlaw who was chasing her easily blocked her escape. Desperate, she swung around again—and found herself facing a second biaquine. It snorted in the confined area, looming above her, the breath from its lowered snout hot against her face. Stumbling back, she looked up. And up. She couldn't see the eyes and nose of the man who sat astride the animal; a cougar helmet hid his upper face. But she saw his mouth. The bastard was *laughing*. He urged his mount closer, backing Janelle up against the biaquine of the bare-headed raider behind her.

Chaos filled the hall. Someone screamed, a cry of terror that abruptly broke off. A short distance away, an outlaw goaded his biaquine to rear and its forelegs pawed the air, smashing a pillar and raining broken tiles over the floor. Farther down the hall, another pillar fell in a cloud of dust and the battle boiled over its remains. The raiders were deliberately ruining the hall, and Janelle could have wept for the destruction of such beauty.

The two outlaws caged her between their mounts. Laughing, the bare-headed man planted his boot between her shoulder blades and shoved her hard into the helmeted man's animal.

"Asshole!" she yelled. The helmeted man reached for her and she socked his arm. Behind her, the other outlaw grabbed a handful of her hair and pulled back her head until she was looking up at him. Exhilaration flushed his face. His yell rang through the clamor, and she thought either he was mad with battle lust or just plain crazy.

Janelle twisted free, but the effort sent her lurching into the other biaquine. It danced to the side and reared, rising far, far too high. Its hooves smashed a column, showering debris everywhere. Gasping, shielding her head, she staggered back, gulping in air. As the biaquine came down, it knocked her over and she fell to the floor, landing hard on her hands and knees. When it reared again, almost directly above her, a scream wrenched out of Janelle.

Scrambling to her feet, she dodged the frenzied animal. The bare-headed outlaw grabbed her again, and this time she didn't fight when he hefted her upward. Better to be caught up there than trampled down here. His saddle was narrow enough that he could throw her stomach-down in front of it, her legs hanging down one side of his biaquine and her torso on the other, with the edge of saddle jutting into her side. Intent on maneuvering his mount among the pillars, he didn't try to hold her down, and she managed to struggle up until she was astride the animal, sitting in front of the invader. She nearly fell in the process, but she kept her seat by holding onto the biaquine.

Calls rang through the mayhem and dust clogged Janelle's nose. The raider kept one arm around her waist, clenching his reins with that hand while he snapped a whip against his mount's flank with the other. She recognized

Dominick's men among the warriors, but the outlaws outnumbered them. Most were no longer fighting; instead, the cretins were trashing the incomparable Fourier Hall.

Then she saw Dominick.

Towering in leather armor, he rode a massive dark animal. He held his sword high, his face harsh with rage. When he shouted, the marauders surged away from him, toward the palace entrance. The first wave reached the entry and flooded out, and Janelle's captor galloped after them.

In the courtyard outside, the clamor lessened, muted by the open space. Almost no one remained to oppose the invaders. Ahead of them, two men on biaquines were forcing along a limping warrior. With a jolt, Janelle recognized the injured man was one of her guards from this morning. His sword arm hung useless at his side and blood pumped from a wound in his shoulder.

An outlaw raised his sword above the bleeding man. In horrified disbelief, Janelle watched the blade descend, flashing in the chill sunlight. She jerked around so she couldn't see, but nothing could shut out the thud of impact or the hideous gurgle that followed.

"Oh, God," she whispered. She prayed it had happened fast enough to spare him pain. She thought of Kadar and her skin felt clammy. Nausea surged over her.

Her captor grunted. "Don't look. It's better if you don't see." He galloped with the other men across earthen courtyards toward the huge wall that should have protected the palace.

Yells broke out behind them. Craning her head to look around, Janelle saw a party of ten men on biaquines racing toward their group from the palace. The outlaws reined in their mounts, throwing sprays of dirt up into the air, and wheeled to face their pursuers. They created a chilling tableau; several hundred raiders confronting a party of ten defenders. The invaders would massacre the palace guards pursuing them.

That was when Janelle sighted Dominick—with the *outlaws*. He sat on his huge dark biaquine at the front of their formation, his gaze intent on the ten men from the palace. The defenders slowed as they came closer, near enough for her to see who led them.

Dominick?

Janelle blinked, looking from Dominick with the raiders to Dominick with the defenders. The Dominick in the small party rode Starlight, the big silver biaquine from yesterday. He wore only trousers and a shirt, with a sword trapped across his back as if he had grabbed it when he was too rushed to don his armor.

The Dominick on Starlight stopped with his party a short distance away from the outlaws. Everyone remained silent, watching while Dominick on the dark biaquine cantered out to meet Dominick on the silver biaquine. Janelle understood then. The brothers were identical twins.

"It's Emperor Maximillian," she said.

"You'd best be silent," her captor answered.

She couldn't fathom how Maximillian could do this to his brother. No wonder the guards had opened the gate. They wouldn't leave the emperor's party milling about outside. They had probably welcomed him, never knowing they were inviting raiders into their midst.

Had Maximillian come to stop the wedding? Supposedly he didn't know. That could mean he also didn't know his men had caught her. Dominick was probably too far away to see her among several hundred riders, particularly since she wasn't the only woman they had taken. But even from here, the fury on his face was plain.

The brothers met in the stretch of dirt between their groups. Their voices carried in the crisp morning air.

"To what the hell *purpose*?" Dominick was demanding. "Do you take joy in killing? Hurting innocent people? Destroying beauty?"

Maximillian lifted his hand, and one of his men rode forward with a rough leather bag that bulged. At the emperor's signal, the man opened the bag and dumped out its contents. Something large fell to the ground and rolled toward Dominick.

A bloody head.

Frozen silence followed the gruesome offering. Then Maximillian said, "Think on this, brother. Next time you send a spy to my army, my response won't be so gentle." His voice hardened. "You were lucky today. We could have killed your servants and burnt your home to the ground."

Dominick bit out his words. "You've spied on me for years."

Maximillian lifted the reins. "If I ordered an attack now, who would stop me? The major portion of your army has been practicing maneuvers. Even riding hard, they won't be here for fifteen minutes. Be wise, Dominick. Fight me and I will retaliate. Is that what you want? No! Leave this land. Go across the sea. Anywhere." He regarded his brother steadily. "Because if you stay, someday I will have to take your life."

The emperor turned then and cantered toward his men.

Dominick reached over his shoulder for his sword. Janelle felt her captor go for his own weapon, and all around her, other raiders were doing the same. When Maximillian saw his men drawing steel, he reined in his biaquine. But he didn't turn to Dominick. He sat in his saddle as if daring his brother to charge and kill him from behind.

Dominick let go of his sword and lowered his arm.

"No!" A woman cried out from within the raiding party. "Prince Dom—" Her voice cut off.

Dominick scanned the riders, his strained expression clear even at this distance. Janelle doubted he could tell who had shouted; even from within the group, Janelle couldn't locate her. The raiders had taken at least fifteen women, probably more. If she called to warn him that his bride was among the captives, she would also be warning his brother.

A way to let him know without revealing herself occurred to her. She was apparently one of the few people he let use his single name. "Dominick!" she shouted. "Here—"

The raider clamped his hand over her mouth. "*Quiet.*"

Janelle clawed at his hand, and he pinned her arms to her sides. Although Dominick looked in their direction, she didn't think he saw her. She struggled to free herself.

"If you make trouble," her captor said, "it will anger the emperor. If he becomes angry, he will retaliate against his brother. And you. He knows this palace. He gave it to Prince Dominick-Michael. He could destroy all of you here. Is that what you want?"

She went still, then shook her head.

Dominick was watching his brother. "Max."

The emperor brought his biaquine around to face him. "We will let the women go when we finish with them."

"This isn't done," Dominick said. "You went too far."

"You have my warning," Maximillian told him. "I give it for our mother's sake, in her memory. But it is the last I will give you."

With that, the emperor wheeled around and set off at a gallop. His men went with him, stirring up a great cloud of dust, pounding out the great gate and away from the palace of shattered arches.

6

MAXIMILLIAN

The raiders followed a trail that switch-backed across the face of a cliff. They rode on the edge of the world, a sheer wall of stone to their left and an abyss of astonishingly clear air to the right, with endless, verdant mountains far below. The line of biaquines clung to the cliff like a fragile string that could snap at any moment.

Janelle saw why Dominick had avoided this route. The path was barely wide enough for one biaquine, with nothing to catch anyone who stepped off the trail. It was also obvious why Maximillian used it; the trail offered a faster path to the flatlands, insurance against Dominick's pursuit when his army arrived to defend their liege.

She shivered as her reaction to the raid set in. She had never witnessed anyone die before, let alone in such violence. It left her raw, mourning for a soldier she hardly knew. Even knowing so little about Othman, she could tell Dominick wasn't ready to take on Maximillian. The ramifications went much further than a violent argument between brothers. Would the people here tolerate a challenge to their emperor? She didn't doubt Dominick would come for the women of his household, but she had no idea how far he would go to rescue them or what he would do when he discovered she was gone.

They kept a grueling pace, and around noon they reached a meadow at the foot of the mountain. The grasses and wildflowers had been trampled earlier, probably by the passage of this same party. Cliffs rose starkly behind them and hilly fields stretched to the south, swirled by yellow and blue blossoms.

The emperor finally called a halt. With a sigh, Janelle's captor reined in his mount. He slid both of his arms around her waist and leaned against her. "Maybe we can get to know each other better now, little bride. You were wanting a man tonight, eh?"

She tried to pull away from him. "Don't touch me."

He dragged back her head and pressed his lips against her neck. But when she twisted in his grip, he didn't wrestle with her. Instead he froze—and released her as if she had a plague. No one paid them any heed; the other men were dismounting, checking biaquines, taking out trail rations. An older man with a gray beard was riding through the group, stopping to confer with various people.

Janelle's captor spoke sharply. "What is your name?"

"Salima." Somehow, she managed to keep the tremor out of her voice. Just barely, but her voice stayed firm.

"You're lying."

She had no chance to answer, for the bearded man had reached them. "How goes it, Aker?" he asked her captor.

"Fair enough," Aker said, his voice cautious.

The other man indicated Janelle. "You can have a few minutes with her. But be ready to ride when the call comes. Maximillian wants to leave the women here, so they don't slow us down."

Aker answered in an oddly subdued voice. "I think His Highness will want to take this one."

Ah, hell. Janelle spoke fast, doing her best to use their dialect. "I'm sick. I'll give a killing fever to anyone who touches me."

The bearded man cocked an eyebrow at her. "You don't look sick to me." His gaze traveled slowly over her. "Far from it."

"I'm in the early stages," she assured him. "The most contagious time."

He snorted. "Which is why you were married today, eh?"

"She's fine," Aker said with a harsh laugh. "You should have seen her in the palace. She screams like a banshee."

Screw you, Janelle thought.

"I will tell the emperor of your offer," the bearded man told him. He continued on to a cluster of other riders.

Aker dismounted and helped Janelle down, but he otherwise went out of his way to avoid touching her. She didn't know whether to be relieved or even more afraid.

The bearded man soon reappeared on foot—accompanied by Maximillian. Janelle's pulse lurched. The emperor could have been Dominick; he had the same eyes, the same strong features, the same height. But unlike Dominick, who warmed with his gaze, Maximillian's stare was ice. He appraised her as if she were an object for sale.

The emperor glanced at the bearded man. "You didn't exaggerate. She is lovely. Exotic, with that yellow hair. Yes, we will keep the bride." He nodded to Aker. "I will remember your generosity."

"Your Highness." Aker sounded strained. "Look at her jewels."

Puzzlement creased Maximillian's face. He pushed Janelle's hair over her shoulder to see her necklace better. For a long moment he stared at it. When he spoke, his voice was too quiet, like the calm in the center of a storm. "Are you my brother's wife?"

Janelle met his gaze. "Yes." She prayed he didn't find out they had never finished the ceremony.

"It *cannot* be. Dominick would never risk his own death to marry some pretty tidbit." He took her chin and turned her face to the side. "My God, you do look like her. But you're too young." His voice hardened. "From where do you come?"

"MIT." She had no idea if it existed here. "Near Boston."

"Boston? What is that?"

"Dominick called it 'another sheet.'"

His posture went rigid. "And your name is Salima?"

She didn't see any point in lying now. "No. It's Janelle."

"Hai," Aker murmured.

Maximillian swore. "That's impossible."

The bearded man spoke. "If she is the one, Your Highness, you have her now instead of your brother."

Maximillian answered with barely controlled fury. "One day. *One day* earlier and I would have been in time." He reached toward Janelle. When she backed away, Aker stepped behind her and grasped her upper arms, holding her in place.

The emperor grabbed several strands of Janelle's hair and yanked them out, making her gasp at the stab of pain. He thrust the tendrils at the bearded man. "Ride to the palace. *Fast.* Have her signature checked. And tell Major Artos to prepare the army. Dominick will soon realize she is gone, if he hasn't already."

Maximillian turned back to Janelle. "You," he said grimly, "will come with me."

The emperor's company rode hard during the day, with stops only to change and rest the biaquines. They continued into the night, lighting their way with torches, the muted roar of their passing rumbling across the hills and then the plains. Maximillian had Janelle sit in front of him on his biaquine. At least he changed his saddle to an animal skin, with its fleece soft against her legs. Smells saturated her senses: leather, sweat, musky animals. Maximillian's armor jabbed her back and his thighs pressed against her hips.

"You know Dominick has five children," Maximillian said when they slowed to rest the horses. "He loved their mother. He hasn't touched another woman since she died. If it wasn't for that godforsaken prophecy, he wouldn't have touched you, either."

Whatever. If he expected to get a rise out of her, he would be disappointed. Her stab of jealousy at his words caught her off guard, but she had no intention of letting him see. When she didn't respond, the emperor spoke tightly. "Dominick will be uncle to your children. Not father."

Janelle didn't realize she was gritting her teeth until she made herself stop so she could talk. Her voice came out like ice. "How noble of you, to rape your brother's wife."

He leaned down, his lips near her ear. "You will regret that."

It no longer surprised her that his men had inflicted such cruelty at the palace. A leader's personality reflected in those who followed him. Yet she also saw Dominick in the emperor; the two men moved alike, gestured alike, spoke alike. Maximillian led his army with the same natural authority and intelligence, and he obviously had the respect of his men. Both he and Dominick exuded an ingrained arrogance that she doubted they were even consciously aware of, though in Dominick it was softened by a sense of humor that suggested he took himself less seriously than his brother.

Some time after the moon began its descent, an officer rode up alongside them, a husky man with well-kept armor. "A messenger has arrived, Your Highness, from the scouts you left to watch the Palace of Arches."

Maximillian didn't look surprised. "Has Dominick come, then?"

"I cannot say. Shall I bring the messenger?"

"Immediately."

As the rider fell back, Janelle's mood lifted like a young bird uncertain whether or not to take flight. Although it seemed unlikely Dominick had already gathered enough forces to come after Maximillian, she could hope.

The officer soon reappeared, accompanied by a red-haired man on a biaquine. Janelle could better tell the difference now between Maximillian's soldiers and the outlaws he had hired to augment his company. This man had the scuffed armor worn by the raiders.

"What is your message?" Maximillian asked.

"It be th' bride." The red-headed man nodded toward Janelle. "The wedding, it never happened."

Janelle silently swore.

Behind her, Maximillian tensed, his arm muscles corded against her skin. "She has his jewels."

"They reversed the ceremonies," the man said. "He gave her the jewels this morning."

Maximillian took Janelle's shoulders and turned her until she could look up at him. "Then you are not yet his."

She met his gaze. "Dominick and I are married."

"My messenger says otherwise." He glanced at his officer. "Go get Brother Anthony."

"But you must have a proper ceremony," the officer protested. "One fit for an emperor. That takes time."

"And give Dominick time to rescue her?" Maximillian said. "I think not. Get Anthony. *Now.*"

"Brother" Anthony turned out to be another craggy, rough-edged warrior with grizzled whiskers and a long scar on his left cheek. He rode alongside Maximillian astride a giant roan biaquine, and the emperor's aides rode with them, surrounding their party on all sides. Their torches cast stark shadows, leaving the faces of the riders half in darkness and half lit by wavering orange light. Anthony wore an unadorned cross, but Janelle couldn't tell if he was a monk, a priest, or a type of cleric that didn't exist in her universe. She just wished she was somewhere else. Anywhere. Like on the moon.

Fleeing the specter of Dominick's pursuit, Maximillian didn't even stop for his own nuptials, but instead kept everyone riding during the entire wedding. He barely even slowed enough for Anthony to speak. So they held the ceremony on the run, as the army rumbled across the plains.

"Each day the sun rises," Anthony droned. "Each night the moon graces the sky in one of its myriad phases, during the ices of winter and the droughts of summer. In the joy of spring or the fertility of autumn, so shall you cleave to each other." He glanced at the emperor. "Maximillian Titus Constantine, do you accept this woman, Janelle Aulair, as your wife?"

"Yes," Maximillian said.

"No," Janelle said.

"No one asked you," Maximillian told her.

"The hell with this," she said. "I'm married to Dominick."

Anthony cleared his throat awkwardly. He produced a scroll from a tube strapped across his back like a sword and handed it to Maximillian. "I've already signed it."

"Seriously?" Janelle demanded, incredulous. "That's *it*?"

"It is done," Maximillian said. "You are Empress of Othman." His voice cut like steel. "And you will learn to respect me, wife, or you will find out just how thoroughly that title can be a curse."

1

FIRE PALACE

The stars glittered as soulless witnesses to the passage of the army. Here in the plains, the night never cooled; even hours past midnight, the air felt like a steam bath. Lines of riders bearing torches wound across the land in rivers of fire.

Janelle dozed, leaning against Maximillian. When she opened her eyes, bleary and confused, the sky had turned crimson. Silhouetted against the horizon, a palace dominated the view. It dwarfed Dominick's home. The central onion dome was surrounded by smaller domes that clustered like great water droplets, gold-plated and glistening. Crenellated bridges arched from tower to tower, glowing in the dawn as if they were flames. The palace shimmered in the morning's fire.

"Do you like it?" Maximillian asked.

"It's spectacular," she admitted.

"It is my home." He sounded tired but satisfied. "And now yours."

The stairway wound around the tower, circling a central shaft of air. Glancing over the railing, Janelle could see all the way to the bottom, many stories below. They were climbing single-file: two guards, Janelle, Maximillian, two more guards. She could barely walk, she ached so much from the ride. Only the unwelcome prospect of being carried kept her from collapsing. Maximillian was a foreboding presence at her back, threatening in his silence and unstated intent.

At least he had no time for her now. The moment they had arrived, people had sought him out: officers, clerks, servants, aides. His advisors were at the bottom of the tower, sorting out what needed to be done, but he obviously had to return to his duties as soon as possible.

Their climb ended at a landing with a heavy wooden door. One of the guards lifted its iron bar and pulled the handle. With a creak of protest, the door swung ponderously open. The guards took Janelle into a circular stone cell with a high ceiling and four small windows, one each looking north, south, east, and west. A large wheel across the chamber was wound with a chain, which then snaked up the wall and across the domed ceiling to its highest point, held in place by iron rings. From the top of dome, the chain hung halfway to the ground. A pair of leather shackles dangled from its end.

Two of the guards went to the wheel, and one tapped a combination into a mechanism there. Leaning their weight into their work, they cranked out the chain. It rattled along the wall, pulled along by its own weight as the shackles descended. A stench of oil permeated the air.

The guards let the chain down to Janelle's height and locked it in place. Another guard pushed her forward, and she stumbled into the shackles, which swung away, then came back and thwacked her shoulder. The entire time, Maximillian watched with an avid gaze.

Janelle gritted her teeth. Two of the guards came up on either side of her, stinking like sweat and biaquines. They lifted her arms over her head and tightened their hold when she tried to pull away. Then they shackled her wrists to the chain.

She stared at Maximillian, her arms held above her body. "*Why?* I've never done anything to you."

"Nothing?" he demanded, incredulous. "You've torn apart my life and destroyed my bond with my brother. That prophecy has brought us nothing but endless grief."

"That may be true. But I have nothing to do with it."

"Of course you do. You *are* it."

"I'm here *only* because Dominick looked for me." She wanted to hurl the words at him. "If Gregor had never said anything, you would have never known I existed." Maximillian and Dominick probably would have been antagonists anyway; they were too much alike, two conquerors in a land that had space only for one.

"You would have come anyway," he said. "When you were seventy."

Janelle doubted it. By that time, he and Dominick would be close to ninety, if they lived that long. Age added a great deal to a person, maybe the serenity of a long life or a cynicism steeped in discord, but whatever happened, surely they wouldn't still be locked in this duel of fates half a century from now. Far more likely, Gregor or the "seeress" had misread whatever created this miserable prophecy.

The guards resumed turning the wheel, this cranking in the chain, and the shackles rose upward, pulling Janelle's arms tight over her head. When the guards continued turning the wheel and she rose into the air, it was too much. She groaned, struggling against the tears that heated her eyes. They locked the chain in place and she hung there by her wrists, suspended in the center of the cell.

Maximillian came over, towering, and stood eye-to-eye with her. "My brother thought he could take my title and my life. He will pay for that." He lifted his riding quirt in front of her. "I shall send this back to him. Soaked with your blood."

Janelle wanted to spit at him. "I don't care how great your title. What you're doing is small. Small and sick."

She expected him to excoriate her with his contempt. But he said only, "A man in my position can never show weakness." Fatigue saturated his voice, revealing an unexpected pain. "For our entire lives," he said, "Dominick and I have been pitted against each other. He must learn I will never tolerate his betrayals. It is true, you will pay the price. That is the way of life."

She regarded him steadily. "He would never do this."

He answered bitterly. "Dominick and his 'moral imperatives.' It is easy for him to preach when he has never sat on an emperor's throne. He grew up flawed by a mother's softness, and now he presumes to suggest I lack a conscience. But inside, he is just like me."

She wasn't buying it. "If he chooses compassion over cruelty, so can you."

Maximillian snorted. "You confuse weakness with compassion."

"Brutality is easy." Her anger sparked. "It takes no strength at all."

A muscle twitched in his cheek. "I will see you tonight." He went to a small table by the door and set down his whip so she would be staring at it. Then he regarded her with an unyielding gaze. "While you are waiting, my empress, it would behoove you to think long and hard about how you speak to me."

Sweat gathered on Janelle's forehead. She was having trouble breathing and her wrists burned from supporting her weight. "You can't leave me like this."

"Why not?"

"I'll suffocate." She struggled to stay calm. "According to the prophecy, if I die, so do you."

He raised an eyebrow, but he didn't refute her statement.

She doubted he would agree to let her down even if he thought she had a good point. He might let a guard do it, though, if he could phrase it in the guise of denying her request. "At least give me the combination," she said. "The one that releases that wheel with the chain." The guards already knew the combination, so he could refuse her by telling them to release it themselves. It was a lame hope, but better than nothing.

Maximillian didn't take the bait. Instead he smiled with condescension. "You couldn't figure out the combination even if I gave you the key."

"Why not?"

"You may be well apportioned in certain aspects." He looked over her body, and her face heated from his rude stare. Then he added, "But I hardly imagine that abstract thought is one of your talents."

Well, screw him. It gave her another idea, though. If he thought she was stupid, he might respond just to taunt her. So she said, "As long as this key of yours doesn't involve math."

He smiled slightly. "What, you don't like numbers?"

She grimaced with distaste. "They don't like me."

"Very well." His arrogant laugh grated. "The combination that releases the chain is the same as the number of terminal zeros in 4089 factorial."

What the hell? She understood what he meant, but she couldn't imagine where that had come from. He had just given her a problem number theory. It wasn't that complicated; middle school students did it in math competitions. But the answer wasn't something most people knew how to find even in her own universe. It wasn't as if much use existed for it outside of math meets. But that suggested Maximillian played games with number theory. Who would have thought? The more she learned about these Constantine brothers, the less she understood them.

The emperor was watching her face. "You do know what a factorial is?"

"No," she lied.

"Pity." He gave a dismissive wave of his large hand. "Not that it would help you. You could never multiply all those numbers together." With that, he motioned to his men. They strode from the cell and the door banged shut, the rumble of its slam vibrating through her prison.

Janelle closed her eyes, exhausted and aching. Then she steeled herself. Damn it, she *would* escape. Who knew if Maximillian's "key" would really give her the combination, but it was no wonder he thought she couldn't solve the problem. To calculate 4089 factorial she had to multiply the first 4089 counting numbers together. No way could she do it in her head.

Except.

She didn't need to know the entire number to figure out how many zeros came at its end. All she needed to know was how many factors of five it contained. Every five, when multiplied by an even number, added a terminal zero. It should be easy. She had done plenty of math games like that. Of course, that was without a megalomaniacal despot inflicting himself on her life.

Janelle concentrated. Dividing 4089 by 5 gave 817 plus a remainder she ignored. She next divided 4089 with 5^2, 5^3, 5^4, and 5^5. When she finished, she added all the results. The first time she came up with 1018 for their sum. That meant 4089 factorial ended in 1018 zeros—if she hadn't made a mistake. She redid it and got 1019. The third time, she came up with 1017. Damn! Why couldn't she get this? It took six tries to convince herself that 1019 was the right answer. All that time, the pain in her arms and shoulders worsened.

"Now what?" she muttered. She had no clue even how to convert the number 1019 into a combination for the lock on the wheel against the wall, let alone any idea of how she would reach the wheel. She stared at the whip on the table, which lay next to several spiked implements she neither recognized nor wanted to. Flinching, she wondered if she would pass out when Maximillian went to work on her. It would be *hours* until night—

No. She clenched her fists in the shackles. He had left her this way because he wanted her to dwell on her fear. So she would think about something else, like how to freaking get out of here. She craned her neck to look around the cell. If she swung as if she were a pendulum, she might reach the wall above the wheel and catch the chain with her foot. From there, she could stretch her leg down to the lock mechanism on the wheel. What exactly she would do if she could manage that contortionist feat remained to be seen.

She kicked her legs to start her body swinging, which worked, but the jerky motion also made her spin at the end of the chain, a dizzying twirl that added to her nausea. The whole time, her absurd clothes chimed, creating far too much noise. The chain twisted until it could wind no tighter and then unwound in the other direction, slowly at first, then spinning her faster and faster. When it finished, it began twisting up the other way. Spin, spin, spin, and all the while she was swinging back and forth. Bloody hell. It was agonizing on her wrists and bile rose in her throat.

Gradually the twisting slowed, winding her up less each time. Finally, mercifully, she came to a rest. Closing her eyes, she breathed slowly until her nausea receded.

Then she tried again.

This time she controlled her swings better. Although the chain still twisted, it spun more slowly than before, enough that she could better direct her swings back and forth in the cell. She finally managed a big enough arc to brush her foot against the wall above the wheel. Her toes scraped the chain but then she swung away, back across the cell. She inhaled with frustration and jerked her body, struggling to make her swing bigger. Back toward the wall, closer—there! She not only scraped the chain with her foot this time, she managed to hook her toes under the metal links. She jerked to a stop—and her foot slipped.

Ai! Away again from the wall, yet another time across the chamber. She would have cursed a blue streak if she hadn't been so out of breath.

After a few moments, her swings slowed to a stop and she hung there, breathing hard. She strained to hear if anyone was outside, but no sound penetrated the thick walls. That worked in her favor; she doubted anyone could hear her bells clanging in here, either. The sun was low in the sky, shining through a window, and she closed her eyes against the glare. She swore at Maximillian's image in her mind—yet it was the same image as the man who had treated her so well the night before. No, it wasn't the same. She would never confuse the cruel lines etched into Maximillian's visage with Dominick's starkly handsome face.

Wetness ran down her arm. Looking up, she saw blood oozing out from under the shackle on her left wrist. It hurt.

Deal with it, she thought, and kicked her legs to swing once more.

This time, she again caught the chain on the wall with her foot. Straining, she held on, her muscles shaking from the exertion. With excruciating care, so she didn't lose her grip, she stretched her other leg out to the wheel. Her big toe scraped the lock mechanism, which consisted of five horizontal levers.

And now?

Janelle had no idea how the levers corresponded to 1019 or if they really even matched at all. For lack of a better idea, she assigned the digits 0 through 9 to the five levers, two numbers for each. Then she pressed out 1019 with her toe. Each time she pushed a lever, it snapped back up into place. Four pushes and she was done.

Nothing.

Gritting her teeth, she reassigned the numbers and tried again. No success. Her third attempt fared no better.

Janelle hissed out a breath. Her foot ached and she couldn't hold on much longer. Frustrated, she smacked her toe across the levers—and they snapped up and down. Hah! They tilted backward as well as forward. Maybe that was how the mechanism accounted for ten digits. She assigned 0 through 9 to all the positions, forward and backward, and retried the pattern, pushing with her beleaguered big toe.

Nothing.

Sweat ran into her eyes. Maximillian had probably made up that story about the combination. *Terminal zeros. Right.* He was the only one of those she had met here. She couldn't quit, though; the alternative was to accept what he intended to do to her. She reversed the order of the numbers she assigned to the levers and pressed the combination yet again—

The lock snapped open.

Whoa! With a squeal of metal, the wheel jerked free from its frozen position and began to unreel. The chain slid madly up the wall, rattling against the stone. Janelle lost her toe-grip on the links and flew back into the center of the cell, all the time dropping as the chain played out. Her feet smacked the ground and she sprawled forward onto her stomach, her shackled arms still over her head. They slammed down in front of her and the clang of metal hitting the stone floor rang through the chamber.

For one moment she lay still, too stunned to move. Then she sat up fast, praying no one had heard the clamor. Euphoria swept over her, followed by an urge to cry, then to laugh. No time to hesitate. She pried at the lock on one shackle, but it didn't budge. With her aching muscles in full protest, she climbed to her feet and limped to the table as fast as she could manage, dragging the chain behind her. Maximillian's whip lay there, coiled next to a belt with metal spikes. She blanched, hoping she never found out how he had planned to use either of those ugly things. She had her own purposes for them, though. She grabbed the belt and worked one of its spikes into the lock on her shackle, prying, pushing, and jabbing, until finally the lock broke open with a loud crack.

As Janelle took off the shackle, more blood oozed over her wrist. Ignoring the lurch of her stomach, she went to work on the other shackle, prying at its lock. With a grating snap, it split open. She dropped the chain and broken shackles, then half limped, half ran across the cell to the closest window. Rising on her toes, she peered through the glass. The window looked north, over the plains where Maximillian's military forces were camped, thousands of men and biaquines, more than she had seen in Dominick's army, more even than she had seen with Maximillian last night. They must have been coming in all day. If she climbed out on this side, anyone down there could see her.

Janelle went to the east window. No more luck there; it also faced the army. In a startling contrast, the south window overlooked a serene garden with a fountain inside the palace. Two women in pale blue and rose-hued silk sat on a bench, chatting and eating fruit. The west window faced a tower that stood above a jumble of courtyards and crooked alleys, all within the palace grounds. She pressed close to the glass and tried to see her own tower below the window. From what she could tell, her prison was in the onion dome of the tower. Its surface outside curved out and down from the window to a ledge that circled the widest point of the onion. The ledge didn't look sturdy, but she saw no better options for escape.

The window, however, refused to open. Janelle ran back to the table with the emperor's Machiavellian implements of pain and swept all that hardware onto the floor. With a grunt, she hefted up the small table and lugged it across the chamber, her sore arms shaking. Summoning what remained of her strength, she swung the table by its legs and slammed it against the window. The pane shattered under the impact, shards of glass flying into the air.

Janelle gulped in a breath and wiped the back of her hand across her forehead, smearing away the sweat. Bending over, she clenched a leg of the table and yanked hard. The blow had weakened its structure, and the leg easily snapped off. She used it to knock away the jagged pieces of glass that remained in the window frame, working with urgency, painfully aware that Maximillian could return any moment.

Within seconds, she had cleared away the broken glass shards. But how to climb out? She considered the three-legged table, then crammed the fourth leg back into the hole left where she had broken it out. Then she flipped the "repaired" table over and set it under the window. When she leaned her weight into its top surface, it wobbled alarmingly.

Pretend it's cemented together, she told herself as she climbed onto the table. It shook and sagged, its broken leg crackling as if summoning its courage to break. Janelle hoisted herself into the window frame, kneeling on the sill she had just scraped free of glass. Tiny shards grazed her skin, but she was secure. Which was good, because below her the table gave an ominous creak and collapsed with a snap of its overtaxed leg.

Calm, she thought. *You're calm. Cool. Collected.* She wasn't fooling anyone, least of all herself, but she kept going. With care, she eased out of the window frame until she was sitting on the curving dome of the tower, balanced high above the world. Wind blew back her hair, and for a heart-stopping instant she felt certain it would knock her off her precarious perch and send her plummeting to the ground below.

Breathe. Deep. Breathe. You'll be fine.

Her pulse slowed. Still sitting, she inched down the bulb, using friction from the soles of her bare feet as brakes. She started to slide anyway, until she thought she would surely lose control, slam into the narrow ledge below, and flip into the air. Gritting her teeth, she dragged her palms on the surface of the dome. It burned her skin, but it slowed her descent. With a jolt, her feet smacked the ledge and she crouched down, fighting for balance, her heart beating like a steam pump.

A breeze clinked the bells on her girdle. She held her breath until her pulse calmed. Then she inched along the ledge toward a decorative span of grillwork that arched from this dome to the next. Far below, an empty alley curved between the towers. After what felt like eons, she reached the arch and climbed onto it, keeping low behind its grill. She crouched there on its narrow span, struggling for breath as if she had been running a marathon instead barely moving.

And now? What next? Janelle took stock of her situation. She was trapped in a place full of people with no reason to help her and plenty not to. She knew nothing about the palace. If she entered any part of the building, she had a good chance of being caught, given how little she knew about anything here. Peering between the scrolled bars of the bridge, she saw a small courtyard below. It contained no people, only a cart built from rough planks of wood with big wooden wheels. Rugs and casks were piled high in its back section.

That inviting courtyard might as well have been miles away. No ladders descended any of the nearby walls, at least none she could see from her hiding place. Her best bet was a wooden trellis that extended up the tower at the end of this bridge. Vines heavy with lush green foliage and red flowers curled around the white latticework. It looked too flimsy to hold a human being, but then, she weighed less than most.

Don't look down, she thought, as if that would somehow make a difference to her weight. She inched along the decorative archway until she reached the dome of the other tower. It curved up to a window high above her, similar to the one in the cell she had just left. She clenched the metalwork of the bridge, steadying herself. Then she clambered over the grillwork where it met the tower wall and lowered herself until she was hanging from the bottom of the bridge. Her right foot scraped the trellis and she hooked her toes into a slat at the top. Straining, she pulled her body over to the framework until she was above the lattice. She concentrated on finding a better foothold and tried to ignore the shaking of her arms.

Her efforts didn't work. She had hung too long in the cell. Her arms couldn't take any more, and as they gave way, she lost her grip. With a gasp, she fell down the trellis. With a desperate grab, she caught framework and yanked to a shoulder-wrenching stop. Immediately she thrust her feet between the slats, taking the weight off her arms. And she clung there, gulping in air as if it were a rarity she might never again find and hoping against all hope that her weight didn't tear the entire structure away from the wall.

Don't stop. She had no time. Clenching her teeth, she resumed her descent. Her world narrowed to the lowering of her body inch by inch. She waited for the trellis to break, for someone to discover her, for that shout of recognition—

Her foot touched the ground.

Janelle collapsed against the wall, heaving in air. She couldn't believe she was down. But she couldn't pause for that rush of relief; voices were coming from where the alley curved around the tower. She darted into a recessed doorway of the tower and knelt in a deep pool of shadow created by the building.

Two men in rough-sewn russet trousers and shirts entered the yard carrying boxes, their sleeves rolled up to their bony elbows. From their conversation, it sounded like they were taking supplies to a monastery. They loaded the cart promptly, with no fuss, and strode back to the palace.

Janelle wasted no time talking herself into her next action; she just ran to the cart. It took only seconds to climb into the back, amid the rugs and burlap sacks of supplies. She had no wish to end up at a monastery supported by Maximillian, but she had even less desire to be here with Othman's notorious emperor. Hiding in this cart might at least give her passage out of the palace. Working fast, she hollowed out a cavity under the rugs, then squeezed in and hauled the heavy carpets over her body, arranging them as much like before as she could manage. Several scratchy bags and a crate poked into her cramped hideaway.

Buried in the sweltering heat, she waited. The darkness grew close and the thick smell of dyed cloth was smothering. Any moment Maximillian would discover her escape and search the area. If this cart hadn't left by then, she would be in more trouble than she ever wanted to imagine. She had been a fool to hide here. She should have snuck into the palace, found some clothes, pretended to be a servant—

A shout came from the courtyard. Her pulse leapt. *Another shout—*

With relief, Janelle realized one of the monks was telling the other to hurry up. Within moments, the cart jolted into motion. She stayed silent, even holding her breath, though she knew, logically, that they couldn't hear her breathe through all these rugs.

A new voice suddenly called out. With a series of jerks, the cart stopped. Conversation trickled into Janelle's hiding place, but she couldn't make out the words. Did Maximillian know she was gone? *Please, let it be something else. Anything.*

Gradually she made out some of the words. A sentry had stopped the cart, a guard who was checking the identification of the two monks. The rumbled exchange among the men seemed to take forever, but finally the rickety cart started moving again. Its wheels creaked, planks groaned, and the rugs whispered against each other all around Janelle. She stayed still, her entire body tensed as they rolled along.

After they had continued for a while at a good clip, Janelle breathed more easily. She parted the rugs a bit, making a spy-hole that allowed her to look outside. They were rolling through the encamped army. It looked endless, soldiers everywhere, with biaquines, oxen, supplies, and the many helpers who tended to the needs of a military force. However, they had been traveling long enough that the sea of people was thinning out. She couldn't see much else through her small hole, only that they were headed toward the mountains.

Janelle covered up the hole and lay still, wrestling with her thoughts. She felt as if she were part of a giant jigsaw puzzle. A prophecy pulled a mathematician from one universe to another; a gate relied on an abstract concept somehow turned into reality; a fabulous hall was named after a mathematician; Dominick understood abstruse theoretical concepts with little background, and his twin also had an unusual knowledge of math. *Why?* She could see the pieces but not the overall picture.

Her stomach growled, a reminder that she had eaten nothing since last night, when Maximillian had shared his trail rations with her. She checked the goods crammed tight around her, several sacks and a crate. The bags held grain. It tasted awful and she disliked taking supplies from monks, but she liked the prospect of starving even less.

She continued her search—and hit gold. Or, more accurately, wine; the crate held ten bottles of a deep red liquid. It took her a while to dig the cork out of one, but she managed. With relief, she drank in gulps, soothing her parched throat. By the time she had finished half the bottle, she felt amazingly content. She had escaped Max the Nightmare, she was still in one piece, and she could almost forget she had no refuge in this bizarre world.

The pain in her wrists was harder to ignore, and she feared the gashes left by the manacles would become infected. Then it hit her: she had an antiseptic. Clenching the neck of her bottle, she poured wine over the cuts. It stung like anything, but after half a bottle of home brew, she wasn't feeling much pain. She opened a second bottle as a reward for her efforts, and soon felt much better . . .

Fire licked her wrists. Flames, heat, burning, burning, *burning.*

Janelle snapped opened her eyes, passing from sleep to waking in a jolt without the usual moment of pleasant nothing. The agony in her wrists made that impossible. Tears wet her cheeks. Whether or not the wine had cleaned her cuts, she couldn't tell, but the gashes hurt like hell.

Another thought jumped into her mind; *where was the cart?* Favoring her wrists, she opened her spy-hole again and looked out. Night had folded over the land with only a flickering glow to light the way, probably from a lamp near the driver. They had left the flatlands with the palace far behind and were rolling through a landscape of low hills that stretched as far as she could see.

Was she safe? Probably not. She doubted she would ever feel safe in this world. Her main concern right now was her injuries. With clumsy hands, she cleaned the cuts on her wrists again. Then she ripped strips of cloth off of a sack and bandaged her wounds as well as she could manage. When she finished, she

drank more wine, a lot more, easing the pain, until eventually she dozed, float-
ing in a sea of flame . . .

Birdsong woke Janelle. Bleary-eyed and hung-over, she peered through her spy-
hole and discovered a rosy, golden dawn lightening the world. The pain in her
wrists had receded. With relief, she closed her eyes again. She dozed more easily
this time, never fully submerged into sleep. Eventually she roused enough to
change her bandages. Dried blood caked the cloth, but the scabs were mercifully
clean, without infection. Then she dozed more.

Sometime in the afternoon, the cart rattled up to a building of dark red stone.
Although Janelle couldn't see much through her hole, what little she could make
out showed her an austere building surrounded by a wall with square towers
at its corners. It fit her idea of a monastery. Voices grumbled nearby, and she
glimpsed two men walking from the cart toward the building.

Janelle waited until the men disappeared from view around the edge of the
high wall. When they were gone, she widened her spy-hole enough to reveal
that the cart stood in a muddy yard paved with stones. Beyond the monastery,
mountains towered into the sky, rough-hewn sentinels not yet softened by ero-
sion. The entire scene had a stark, austere beauty that made her breath catch.

Moving stiffly from her cramped sleep, Janelle pushed aside the rugs and
climbed out of the cart, easing to the ground by the huge spoked wheel. Her
head swam and she sagged against the cart with a groan, using its wheel for
support.

Voices came from the east side of the building where the monks had disappeared. Startled, Janelle pushed herself upright and took off in a limping run
toward the west side of the monastery. She dodged onto a narrow path there
that squeezed between the high wall and a muddy hillside. Her vision blurred,
but she kept going, holding as many of her bells against her body as she could
manage and hoping no one heard the infernal clinking of those she couldn't
reach.

She came out behind the monastery. The roughly-mortared wall sported two
entrances, each a wooden door with big iron braces. She crossed to the first one,
keeping watch on the area all around. This place was apparently isolated enough
to lull its inhabitants into a sense of security, because the door wasn't locked. It
opened on a storeroom stacked with crates, which looked innocuous until she
realized a storage area was exactly where she *didn't* want to be if the monks were
about to unload the cart. She slipped back outside and ran to the second door.
This one let her into a foyer, a small square area with a staircase to the right.
After silently easing the door closed, she limped over to the stairs and climbed
them, taking care to make no noise. She came to a landing where they turned
right and sunlight slanted through a round window on the left wall. She paused
to stare out the window, surveying the area. It looked onto a walled quadrangle
in the center of the building, a yard open to the sky.

Janelle tensed. Three men were crossing the yard. Monks maybe, but they didn't fit her image of such holy men. Instead of robes, they had on trousers, scuffed work boots, and simple white shirts. They seemed more like laborers than religious types. She held still, uncertain. Did she dare ask the people here for sanctuary? Maybe not. She doubted they wanted to provoke Maximillian, particularly in the matter of this odious prophecy.

Janelle let out a breath and continued on, climbing the stairs up to another landing, this one with a door. She leaned into the barrier, listening. Nothing. Whatever lay beyond this door involved no voices, noises, or other indications that people were about. Edging it ajar, she peered through the opening. A long hall stretched out on the other side. And empty hall.

"Okay," she whispered. So far, so good. She limped down the hall to the first door and stopped to listen. *Not* so good. Voices rumbled beyond the barrier, at least two men talking, maybe more. She backed away, casting her gaze about the corridor, and moved on. At the next door, silence greeted her. So. What to do? Take the risk, open the door, see if she could hide inside, or stay outside and risk being seen if someone left another room or came down the hall.

Janelle opened the door. Inside, she found . . . a library. An *empty* library.

Yes! With a silent exhale, she stepped inside and closed the door. A large hook jutted out from the wall to her right and a big skeleton key hung from the curve of metal. It turned out the key locked the door. Secure inside, she looked around her refuge. It had a cozy, well-used look. In the center, a long table took up a lot of room, built from a polished dark wood with carvings of leafy vines around its edge and on its legs. The three chairs around it were in the same style, as was the banquette against the opposite wall, except for the blue embroidered cushions on its seat. A window above the bench let sunlight slant into the room, and dust motes danced in the golden shafts.

Janelle crossed to the bench and leaned over it to look out the window. The pane was locked but she could see the quadrangle, empty now except for vegetable plots and apple trees. The monks she had seen earlier were nowhere in sight. For at least this moment, she was safe.

With a sigh, she sunk down on the bench and sagged back against the wall behind it. She gazed around the library, at its antique furniture and parquetry floor. Despite its worn condition, it was beautiful, but what compelled her the most were the *books*. Shelves lined every wall from floor to ceiling, each of them lined with old-fashioned tomes.

"Can you all help me escape this place?" she said wistfully. The weathered appearance of the room suggested that either the monks had forgone the proverbial material wealth or else they had lousy financial support. She fingered the coins on her girdle. She was a walking treasure trove, what with all the noisy gems and precious metals she was wearing. Maybe she had some bargaining power. She could offer them payment to send for Dominick. Then again, Maximillian would probably reward anyone who returned his wife, and she doubted her bangles had much value compared to his wealth. Nor were her jewels likely enough to tempt these people if they thought helping her would piss off their odious emperor.

Janelle raked her hand through her hair. She needed to know more about how things worked here. She went to a shelf and pulled out a book at random. The text had an odd title: *Elektron Motion: Antique Editions, Monografs of Rekord. Elektronik form: Alhambra Graphiks.*

The publication date was 1546 A.D.

She squinted at the cover. If dates were the same here as in her world, this book was centuries old. Electron Motion? That sounded like atomic theory. *From 1546 A.D.?* The title implied it was a collector's monograph, an "antique" book created from an electronic publication. Given everything she had seen in this world, the existence of that level of technology five centuries in the past made about as much sense as cave men with cell phones.

Then again, these people could step between universes.

She flipped through the book. A preserving finish protected its paper pages, which would have probably otherwise fallen apart with age. Reading wasn't as difficult as she expected, despite the odd spellings; physics was physics regardless of language. The first chapter dealt with electronics and the second with an electron gas. A chapter on electrochemistry followed, then one on the quantized energy levels of an atom. Unlike texts in her world, which treated those topics as different subjects, here they were lumped into one text on "elektron motion."

She replaced the book on its shelf and took another text from nearby. This one was even older than the last, with a publication date of 1489 A.D. It discussed the physics of heat flow. Although the models differed from those in her world, they gave the same results: heat came from molecular motion and was a form of energy.

"My God," she murmured. How could this be? She pulled out a fat tome titled *Dynamical Analysis*. The first half of the book focused on her specialty, the solution of advanced partial differential equations. The rest of the book presented applications of the math to physics problems dealing first with the classical motion of particles and then delving into semi-classical models of molecular behavior. More urgent now, she set the book on the table and pulled out more tomes, searching specifically for science texts. The books she found all followed the same form as the first two, opening with chapters on mathematical theory followed by applications. A treatise on genetics described how biaquines had been bioengineered from horses for strength, speed, and the ability to fight.

Then she found a book on tensor analysis.

By themselves, tensors were just arrays of numbers. Nothing unusual. But they appeared extensively in certain sciences, including general relativity. Einstein's bailiwick. Einstein had believed it was impossible to travel faster than light, a result that would limit the ability of humans to visit other star systems in their lifetimes. The theory described here resembled his work, but with one difference—this author assumed faster-than-light travel existed. A chill ran through Janelle. This read like a historical text, one written *after* the advent of such travel.

She began a methodical search then, and it didn't take long to find what she sought, what she didn't believe would actually exist until the moment she opened the book. Titled, simply, *Advanced Formulations*, its chapters covered wormholes, space warps, and complex speeds that circumvented the singularity at light speed. One section presented resolutions to the paradoxes for super-luminal travel, including a discussion of alternate spaces and times. It proposed a "Riemann screen" that could offer views of those other continuums. It was then that she understood: the "Jade Pool" of the prophecy was a viewing portal into alternate universes. The prophecy that Gregor had revealed to the emperor must have come from a timeline he observed in a different universe using a Riemann screen.

The final chapter detailed the design of a faster-than-light starship drive.

Janelle sat at the table, surrounded by books, too stunned to read more. These people had achieved interstellar travel *five centuries ago*. What the blazes had happened since then?

Footsteps sounded outside.

Janelle froze. A door opened nearby, then closed. She glanced around, frantic, but saw nowhere to hide. As the doorknob to the library turned, she jumped to her feet and her clothes jangled. The knob rattled as someone tried to open the locked door.

The footsteps receded.

Janelle hurried to the window and tried to open it, then banged on the glass. Nothing worked. She went to the door and leaned against it, straining to hear what was outside.

More footsteps.

She backed up until the table stopped her retreat. A key clinked in the lock.

No. To have come this far, to have made this incredible discovery, only to be caught—*no, not now.*

The door opened.

8

PROPHESIER

A slender man stood in the archway. Wrinkles surrounded his eyes and he wore his grey hair long, in a queue pulled back from his face. His clothes were simple, brown trousers and an unadorned gray shirt. He stared at Janelle, his mouth slightly open showing a row of even if slightly yellowed teeth. Then he drew in a breath, stepped inside, and quietly closed the door.

"This is an odd place for a bride," he said.

She folded her arms over her skimpy clothing, covering her stomach. "I need to contact my husband."

"I've seen that girdle," he said coldly. "The emperor's aunt wore it at her wedding. So will the bride of the emperor's brother."

"Yes, I'm Prince Dominick-Michael's wife." In truth, she had no idea who she was married to, but she wasn't about to tell him that. "I need to send him a message."

He spoke dryly. "And why, pray tell, are you in a monastery, alone, hundreds of miles from any city, on your wedding day?"

Good question. Too bad she couldn't give a good answer. "It's not my wedding day."

"Why else would you dress that way?"

"The wedding already took place."

"Who hurt your wrists?"

She covered the bandages on one wrist with her hand. "I must go to Dominick."

He lifted his chin. "This monastery serves the emperor. We will send for him."

"No! You can't do that."

His gaze narrowed with suspicion. "We are loyal servants to Maximillian. If his brother needs to be contacted, the emperor will do so."

"I can offer you a reward." Inspiration came to her. "One worth far more than jewels or gold." She indicated the books on the table. "I can tell you what these mean. It could improve your lives beyond imagining." Whether she could actually do that was debatable, but she had no doubt she could offer him more than he knew now, if the level of understanding she had so far seen in this world accurately portrayed how little the people here retained of their ancient knowledge.

The monk snorted. "That is hard to believe."

She met his skeptical gaze steadily. "But true."

"Prince Dominick-Michael would never marry any woman except the one from the prophecy." His voice hardened. "And, Lady Janelle, the emperor would do anything to prevent that marriage."

Damn. "You seem to have decided who I am. You have me at a disadvantage."

"I am Gregor."

Gregor? Her pulse surged. "You're the one! *You* made that ghastly prophecy." She lifted her arms out from her sides, palms to the ceilings, fingers pointing to all the books. "You figured out enough here to look across space and time, right? But you don't really understand it, do you? Otherwise, you could have told them more." She scowled at him. "Like how it works."

His jaw stiffened. "I have spent my entire life studying these books. I understand them better than anyone else alive."

She plunged ahead, ad-libbing. "That's why I'm the prophecy." For all she knew, it was true. It was no more bizarre than anything else that had happened here. "I was sent to you, Brother Gregor. Would you like to know more? Give me sanctuary and I'll tell you."

His angry stare turned incredulous. "You think I would betray Othman in my own lust for knowledge?"

For crying out loud. "A love of knowledge is a gift. Not an undesirable lust."

He frowned at her. "You talk a great deal."

You bet I do. "Think what you could learn. You're a brilliant scholar; you must be, to have tamed space and time." She didn't know him, but if he understood even a small part of these books with no formal training, it could be true. "I can help unlock these mysteries for you."

"You speak *blasphemy*." He cut the air with a sharp wave of his hand, palm out, as if he would dismiss her from his sight and mind. "Such study is for men, and only those who dedicate their lives to the monastery, forgoing riches, prestige, *and* women."

"A lot of these books have female authors."

He glared at her. "That may be. But living women aren't allowed in here." His gaze traveled over her body and he flushed, then made an obvious effort to pull his attention back to her face. "You will not seduce me into betraying the emperor."

"For flaming sake," she said. "What betrayal?" She clenched her fists, ignoring the pain in her wrists. "You think it's all right for Maximillian to kidnap his brother's wife, hang her up by shackles, and threaten to torture her, but heaven forbid she should try protect herself?"

"I don't claim Maximillian is a gentle man." He stepped back to the door and pulled a cord hanging there. "But he is my master and I am sworn to obey his word and law."

Janelle felt the blood drain from her face. "What does the cord do?" When he didn't answer, her anger sparked. "Was it a game to you, pitting Maximillian and Dominick against each other from the day of their birth?"

"No." An unexpected fatigue showed on his lined face. "It threatens all I value. The well-being of Othman."

"And you think that well-being depends on me going to Maximillian?"

"He is the emperor." Gregor pulled himself up straighter. "It is my moral duty to act in his best interest."

She crossed her arms. "How can you talk about moral duty when you intend to send me to be brutalized by a monster?"

"I hardly think you are fit to pass judgment on an emperor."

"Why not? I know brutality when I see it."

Gregor shifted his weight. "How he treats you and how he rules Othman are different matters."

"Like hell."

"At your age and with your female attractions—" He cleared his throat awkwardly. "You don't have what it takes to make such judgments."

Where did he come up with this stuff? "I may be young," she said, "but that doesn't mean my brain doesn't work. And what on Earth does you finding me sexually attractive have to do with my ability to think?"

His face turned red. "You twist my words."

"No, I don't." Frustrated, she said, "You make it sound as if I'm evil because I don't want to go back to a man who plans to thrash me until my blood soaks his whip."

"I have to do what I believe is right. I cannot sacrifice higher principles for your welfare."

Her gaze never wavered. "I question the validity of your principles."

"If my principles weren't *valid,* it wouldn't have mattered to me whether or not you had reason to remain in your cold, soulless universe. You had no one there. Nothing."

"What?" Janelle stared at him. He couldn't mean what she thought. He *couldn't.*

His voice quieted. "I saw them die. The nobleman in Andalusia. His lady. Their son." With unexpected sympathy, he added, "Your family. I am sorry."

The air seemed to rush out of the room. "He wasn't a nobleman." She felt as if the world had suddenly gone quiet. "He was an ambassador. He was making bridges among different peoples. Finding a way to peace through understanding. How can you call that soulless? My family *died* for that dream."

"I respect such a dream." He straightened out his shoulders. "But no matter what their hopes, in the end, they left you alone."

She couldn't answer. Too much pain lay on that path.

Footsteps sounded in the hall. They stopped, and the doorknob turned. Four men entered the room, all dressed like Gregor, two with greying hair, the other two younger, brawnier.

Turning to them, Gregor said, "We have a guest. We must send word to the emperor."

* * *

The monks gave Janelle a shawl she could wrap around herself, though she suspected they did it more for their own peace of mind than for her. They locked her in a high corner room, provided water and a basin, and brought her fruit, cheeses, and a carafe of wine. Then they left her alone.

As demoralized as she felt, she was ravenous. She wolfed down the food, then washed up and searched her cell. Shaped like a piece of pie, it measured five paces by three at the wide end. The walls were white-washed plaster. A bench stood against the outer wall, and above it, light trickled in a window slit. Swirls on the cloudy glass reminded her of the Mandelbrot fractal. Had Dominick's ancestors learned chaos theory? *What secrets were locked in that library?*

She was still reeling from what Gregor had told her. He saw her family die. It was part of what convinced him that she was destined to come here. She knew he couldn't have affected what happened through the Riemann screen, that he might not have even seen their actual deaths, only that horrific news clip of the car exploding. But nothing would stop the pain that flooded her.

To distract her painful thoughts, she tried escaping. She rapped the walls, prodded, scraped, pushed, yanked anything she could reach. She pounded the window, trying to break the glass, even knowing she couldn't wriggle out the narrow opening. It offered a view of the yard that fronted the monastery—and so she saw when the riders left, galloping down the same trail the cart had taken up here. She thought of Maximillian and felt ill.

Eventually, she sank onto the floor in one corner and pulled her knees to her chest. Laying her head on her knees, she closed her eyes and gave in to her exhaustion.

Janelle awoke with sunlight slanting across her face. A clamor outside had roused her: men were calling to each other, biaquines trumpeting, boots stamping. Muzzy with sleep, she climbed onto the bench and peered out the window. Warriors filled the slice of the yard she could see, large men in armor with heavy weapons, some on foot, others astride dark biaquines.

And Maximillian.

He strode across her field of view, his black armor absorbing the sunlight, his dark hair whipping around his face.

"No!" She scraped at the window, trying desperately to dig out the glass. Only a sliver of stone crumbled under her assault. She kept going, knowing it would take hours to dislodge the window, knowing she could never fit through the opening anyway. But she couldn't quit. She remembered the shackles, the whip, the spikes, and the ugly hunger in his gaze.

Behind her, a key turned in the lock.

9

THE KEY

Janelle spun around, facing the door. As she jumped off the bench, she pulled the shawl around her body, as if that paltry covering could somehow shield her.

The door creaked and swung heavily inward. Gregor stood in the opening, regarding her with an impassive face. Maximillian towered in the shadows behind him, the hilt of his giant sword jutting above his shoulder. The clanks and calls of the soldiers outside the window sounded muted, distant, and the air smelled of dust.

For a long moment, Gregor stared at her, his expression impossible to read. Finally he stepped aside and turned, then executed a deep bow to the emperor. Maximilian gave him the barest nod. With that, Gregor left them, his footfalls receding down the hall. Maximillian remained, his unsmiling gaze fixed on Janelle. With a slow tread, he walked into the cell—

And it wasn't him.

"*Dominick!*" Janelle flung herself across the room, and he caught her in an embrace. She wrapped her arms around his waist and laid her head on his chest, closing her eyes while tears squeezed out under her lids.

"Ai," he murmured, stroking her hair. "I wasn't sure what to expect. I feared you must hate me."

"I don't hate you." Her voice caught. "I hate what you've done to my life."

He drew back to look at her, holding her shoulders in his big hands. "I swear, my brother will never hurt you again. *Never.*"

She felt dizzy with the release of fear. "Gregor told me he was sending for Maximillian."

"Whatever you said convinced him to seek me instead. His men found my army *en route* to Max's palace." Unexpectedly, he laughed. "You have sorely traumatized our dear Brother Gregor. He informs me that you are a most disturbing woman. He says he does not envy my marital state."

She managed a smile. "Trauma builds character."

"So it does." His amusement faded. "I will leave my Sixth Regiment here. You and I can ride home with the rest of my army."

From what Janelle had gathered, only twenty men lived at the monastery, scholars rather than warriors. "Do you really need so many soldiers to counter a few monks?"

"Not to counter. To protect. In summoning me, they have risked Maximillian's wrath."

"Do you think they'll be all right?"

"I think so, as long as my men are here." He held out his hand. "Come home with me, Janelle."

She took his hand.

The library in Dominick's palace awed Janelle. It old, ancient even, kept up through the centuries by Dominick's family. She wandered through room after room, feeling as if she had found a place of enchantment. Bookshelves lined every wall, stretching from the gleaming parquetry floors up to a vaulted ceiling inlaid with geometric mosaics in gold, green, and red. Engravings in the wood curved in vine motifs, and marble panels between some of the shelves bore quotes from scholars she didn't recognize. Gold and burgundy brocade upholstered the armchairs. Tall lamps stood in the corners, flickering with flames behind their stained glass shades. Most of all, books filled the rooms, embossed, gilt-edged, glossy everywhere in the golden light. Sliding ladders gave access to the upper shelves. Whoever had built this place had valued its contents above anything else she had seen here.

Janelle's bodyguards stayed back, giving her a semblance of privacy. She had barely spoken to Dominick during the ride here from the monastery. She needed to sort out her thoughts. Nor did she know what to say to him; they had so little in common. Yet he stayed on her mind. It was more than her undeniable physical attraction; he also intrigued and compelled her. But she wasn't ready for this formidable man who would be emperor.

Perhaps he understood. He hadn't insisted on accompanying her here. He had to know she was avoiding him; having his bride immediately seek out his library upon arriving at her new home was hardly the most romantic behavior. Then again, most brides hadn't just discovered the world's most stunning trove of knowledge. The books in the monastery were so far beyond anything she had expected, it overshadowed even her shock at finding herself in Dominick's universe.

Although her new husband seemed puzzled by her excitement over what he considered some old books, he didn't resist her determination to read them. At first she just wandered through the rooms of the library, taking it all in. Judged from the most modern scrolls, the year here corresponded to the year in her universe. This was their version of the early twenty-first century. So strange.

However, just as in Gregor's library, the science and math sections here had no recent books. The texts were centuries old, the most recent dated 1557 A.D. A layer of dust covered them. They were just as advanced as the ones she had found at the monastery, except the collection here was larger and more extensive. Even stranger, she found no *history* of science, no explanation of how these people had once possessed such great knowledge and now had so little.

In fact, she found few histories of any kind, though she searched for over an hour. Several ornately embossed tomes described the reign of Dominick's family in great detail, but they didn't go back as far as the sixteenth century. Although the historical accounts were harder to read than the math or science books, she could tell they focused on wars and politics, what the authors considered the great deeds of the Constantines. Yet she found many hints that his ancestors had also distinguished themselves in scholarly pursuits, showing that same gift for abstract thought she had seen in Dominick and Maximillian.

One section of the library dealt with architecture, including discussions about the Palace of Arches. None of them explained the Fourier Hall, at least not as far as she could decipher from the unfamiliar language. However, a few studies mentioned a "key," referring either to that great hall or else to the arches themselves. She kept looking for more, but nothing in the history section helped.

It was a military text of all places, a book on ancient war codes, where she finally found the answer. One of its chapters included a lengthy discussion on the "Key of Arches." She took the big tome to an armchair and settled in to read, pouring over the text, puzzling out the words. Yes, it was becoming clear. The arches of that gorgeous hall formed a code. Their Fourier transform was a key.

A key to *what*?

Janelle sat back, thinking. In two dimensions, the transform would probably look like a narrow peak with rippled tails; in three dimensions, it might resemble the diffraction pattern for a circular aperture, like a circular hill surrounded by smaller circular ridges. From what she understood of the text, the locations of that central peak would specify a time. For what? The book described a *portal* of some kind. It wasn't the Riemann gate that had brought her to this universe, but a gateway to some event.

A big event.

Janelle moved her chair to an antique desk with scrolled sides, a rollback top, and gilded edges. She rummaged in its drawers until she found an ink bottle, quill, and several sheets of parchment. It took her a while to figure out how to use the quill, but eventually she set to work, intent on deriving the Fourier transform of the arches. She couldn't do it exactly; that would require a computer. But she could figure out a reasonable approximation. The book gave drawings and measurements for the hall, and she modeled the arches as the sum of a few squared sine waves.

As she ground away at the equations, the lamp behind the desk burned low. Gradually she found the solution she sought. When she was fairly sure she had done it as well as was possible without a computer, she drew the resulting transform as a mathematical curve. The shape was what she had expected, a large peak in the center with smaller peaks on either side rippling away. The big peak was centered at the number 2057. Why? The book implied it referred to time. Could it be 2057 years in the future or the past? The year 2057 AD? What?

A chill went through Janelle. In 2057, she would be seventy-one, the age of the woman in the prophecy. This *couldn't* connect to her—for that implied she would be here in fifty years.

Dismayed, she went on another search, delving again into the science section of library. She checked every shelf, knelt on the polished wooden floors to check those at the bottom and climbed the ladders to search the topmost shelves. She scoured every section she could find with science texts, especially physics, and math.

And finally she hit gold.

The book, titled "Ancient Legends and Sciences," included a modern account of the Jade Pool, one written twenty years ago. The "jade-hued surface" it described sounded exactly like the Riemann screen she had read about at the monastery. The author considered the "pool" an enigmatic artifact of mythical proportions and presented the equations that described its operation as if they were the runes of a spell. It helped Janelle fully appreciate just what Gregor had achieved, if he had managed to unravel practical knowledge from such fanciful treatments.

The book also discussed Riemann gates, which turned out to be a more complicated application of the screen. Apparently such a gate had brought her to this universe. She didn't understand the technology, but she could work through the math. And she did, in detail. Over and over. Yet no matter how many times she redid her calculations, no matter how many times she checked for mistakes, she always derived the same result: the gate didn't depend on two sheets—it involved *hundreds*. Dominick had managed to go back and forth to her universe three times, but now that gate had closed and the entire cycle would have to complete before it reopened. That would take centuries, maybe even millennia.

Janelle stared at the parchment with its blotted ink. Centuries. Millennia. It might as well be forever. She folded her arms on the desk and put her head on her forearms.

Some time later, a man spoke gently, his voice a deep rumble. "Janelle?" A big hand rested on her forearm.

She lifted her head to find Dominick watching her. The lamps in the library had burned low, leaving her in a pool of antique-hued light around the desk. Dominick had pulled up one of the tiled stools from the library over the desk and was sitting next to her.

"What happened?" he asked.

She shook her head, too disheartened to answer.

"Tell me," he said softly.

Her voice caught. "I don't think I can go home." The words hurt. "If you hadn't opened the gate when you did, you could never have found me. I would have been long dead before the cycle returned to my universe."

He stared at her, his eyes large in the flickering lamplight. "Are you telling me the prophecy created itself? That if Gregor had never spoken, you wouldn't be here?"

She could only say, "Yes."

He answered in a low voice. "Then I am doubly sorry."

"Something happens in fifty years," she said unevenly. "When I'm the age of the woman Gregor saw in the pool. Another gate is going to open. A *big* one. During those few months, your people can do something huge." She held back her tears. This was too important to Dominick and his people for her to lose it now. "Something incredible."

He seemed bewildered. "What something?"

"I'm not sure." Janelle spoke slowly. "I don't believe your ancestors meant to strand you here forever without technology." She laid her palm against his chest. "Your family had the keys to understand once. You can find them again."

A strange look came into his dark eyes. "There is a saying."

"A saying?"

"This." He spoke in an unfamiliar tongue, words with an ancient sound, almost a chant, exotic and eerie in the gilded light of this library out of space and time.

"What does it mean?" she asked.

"Roughly translated, it says 'Constantines are the key to the future.'"

The key to the future. He, the prince of the Hall of Arches, might have the keys he needed here within his own palace. "Who else besides you and the monks has a library like this, with the ancient books?"

"Just Maximillian. His is even larger than mine."

Maximilian. The Constantine emperor who liked number theory. "My God," she whispered. "It's *you*. Your family. *You're* the keys. The Fourier Hall is a clue or a remnant, like the waveforms on so many of the walls here, but you are the guardians of the knowledge. It's probably why your family ended up ruling Othman." She motioned at the library around them. "Everything you've lost is still here. The ability to unlock it is *in* you, in your genes, your minds. If you can find it." She felt as if she were breaking. "But why me? How could you reach across universes for someone to help you do this?"

He spoke in a subdued voice. "Gregor said the pool showed many futures. My father wanted the one that maximized his empire. I always assumed it depended on who ruled, Max or me, and that you came into it because you brought power into our family, probably through an alliance." Quietly he said, "Perhaps this is much larger than a battle between brothers. It may be something only you can do."

A tear slid down her face. "At what price?"

"Ai, Janelle." He drew her to him. "I don't know how to take you home. But if you let me, I will give you a home here worth having."

She laid her head against him and fought back her tears.

Dominick's suite was far different than the chamber where Janelle had spent her first night in the palace. For one, it was five times the size. Low, black-lacquered tables stood on tasseled carpets strewn with big cushions. The rugs he used for a bed filled one corner, tumbled with velvet pillows, and two huge crossed swords hung on the wall above it, their hilts inlaid with topazes. Tapestries in gold, red, and green hung on the walls. Braziers burned in the corners of the room and oil lamps flickered in wall sconces, shedding a dim golden light over the scene. It all had a barbaric elegance.

Janelle sat with Dominick on his bed, leaning against the wall. They had come here from the library, and now he held her close in his arms, fitted to his side. She laid her head against his shoulder, her thoughts edged with pain, and for a long time they simply sat together in the dusky light.

Eventually Janelle spoke. "It's hard to believe you are brothers."

He answered in a low voice. "Do not see me with blinders. What Max does, what he believes, the way he sees that world—that is all within me as well. I had a different life and it taught me other ways, but had brutality molded me instead, I would be just like him."

"But you aren't like him."

"I hope not, at least in the ways that matter."

"Will you go to war?"

Dominick let out a tired breath. "He is my brother. Despite everything, he is my only close kin. It may even be that I still love him." He raked his hand through his hair. "But I will not desert my people to go 'across the sea,' as he says I must. If that means we must fight, so be it."

She understood. Six of his officers had died in the raid on the palace. He could rebuild the hall, but nothing would bring back those men. At least Kadar, the guard who had helped her in the tunnels, had survived. He had been injured, but he was recovering.

After a while, Dominick said, "Gregor told me about your family. I am sorry."

She couldn't talk about that loss, still so raw in her memory. So she said only, "My father was an ambassador. Do you have them here?"

"Yes. It is a position of honor, usually held by a nobleman." He rubbed his hand along her upper arm. "The people of Othman have a history of strife with the Andalusian Empire. We descend from their colonies but we gained our independence centuries ago."

Andalusia. Southern Spain. "The empire doesn't exist in my universe. Spain is a nation, though. I lived there for years, when my father was ambassador."

He didn't seem surprised. "It is no wonder the prophecy predicted you would affect our balance of power. Your background suits you well to the throne."

Dryly she said, "I don't think your brother was interested in my background."

Dominick grunted. "Max will never be satisfied until he takes you from me or kills us both. He will succeed with neither."

"He says he and I are married."

Ire sparked in his voice. "He cannot marry my wife."

"His spy told him you and I never wed."

"I gave you the jewels," he growled. "And we consummated the marriage. So we are wed."

"Uh, Dominick." She lifted her head to look up at him. "We didn't consummate it."

"I stayed the night. As far as anyone knows, we did." He cleared his throat. "Unless you plan to say otherwise."

She smiled. "I won't."

His shoulders relaxed. "Good."

"I met your daughter. She's charming."

His tone gentled. "Yes. All my children are."

"I'm sorry . . . about their mother."

"Ah, well." He seemed muted somehow. "It has been years."

He fell silent after that, and she regretted bringing up the memories. After a moment, she asked, "What happened to your people five hundred years ago? Was there a war? A catastrophe?"

"I don't think so." For one of the few times since she had met him, he sounded uncertain. "Some of the people just, well—left."

"To where?"

Dominick pointed upward. "There. Somewhere." He spoke thoughtfully. "I have more education than most because my mother insisted that Max and I study history, language, astronomy, and mathematics when we were boys, as much as anyone could teach us. But it barely touches what is in my library. Why did our ancestors desert this world and never come back?" He shook his head. "We have lost that knowledge. They took so much with them. Legend says they left us behind deliberately. Some claim a political rift existed between those who went and those who stayed. Others say we remained of our own free will, as guardians of Earth, and that those who left cannot return because they became lost between worlds, even universes." Softly he said, "Perhaps it is both. But it's been half a millennium. Our memories are faded."

It was heartbreaking to think of the human race fractured that way. "They *are* going to return. I'm not sure how or where or why, but I'm certain it happens in fifty years."

"An astonishing thought."

"It will change your world."

"So after all these centuries, we made have an answer to this ancient puzzle, when we will see our brethren again." He considered her. "This answer of yours creates more questions than it solves."

"I know." She thought back to the library. "The answers are here. I'm sure of it."

"You will search for them?"

She nodded, gratified he didn't object. "Gladly."

"You say I have some small talent for scholarly pursuits." He seemed bemused.

"More than small, I think."

"I haven't the interest, though." His smile flashed. "But ah, Janelle, our children will be brilliant."

Children. She would have his children. A startling thought, that, though not unwelcome, she discovered. But it hurt to realize her children would never know her world. It was true what he said, though; if their children inherited their parents' ability for abstract thought and learned to use it, they might truly reach for the stars.

She would teach them what she knew. Most of all, she would love them, as her parents had loved her.

Dominick was watching her face. "Together, you and I can achieve much."

"I hope so." Her voice caught. "We will make a good place." Somehow.

"Aye," Dominick murmured. "We will."

Janelle didn't know if she would ever fully understand this complicated man, but she wanted to try. Life here wouldn't be easy. It was a violent world, harsh and unyielding, and Maximillian would always be there. Yet it also had an incredible beauty. If she could never go home, she could at least have her work in the library, a family to love, and dreams of the day when humanity might one again soar beyond the bounds of Earth, a dream she would never have hoped to realize in her own universe.

A bittersweet peace settled over her. This wasn't a life she would have chosen. But it might hold joy, even astonishing events, and for that, she could look forward to the future.

LIGHT

AND

SHADOW

INTRODUCTION

"Light and Shadow" came to me at a time when I had no idea if I was any good as a writer or if I would ever be published. Back then, it was so frustrating to write and write, sending out stories, going for that seemingly unattainable acceptance, always afraid I was stumbling over my metaphorical feet. When I submitted this story to *Analog*, I wrote the editor Stan Schmidt a too long cover letter explaining the theoretical physics behind the plot. I was so green back then, I didn't know I was breaking rules, wasting an editor's valuable time, that I should let the story speak for itself.

I was lucky. Stan had an interest in the subject. He answered my query with a gracious letter commenting on the physics, telling me about some of his work, and gently pointing out problems with my story. He finished the letter with that sentence unpublished writers have coveted since editors first began publishing us. He said if I could fix the problems, he would be interested in seeing the story again.

Nervous and excited, I did my best to make the fixes. I sent back the revised, and this time I had enough sense to be sparing with details in the cover letter.

He accepted the story for publication.

Publication!

"Light and Shadow" was my first story in *Analog*, my first story in any magazine, the first published story about the Ruby Dynasty, and one of the first I ever wrote. It has always been special to me, also the first story about Kelric, a character who figures prominently in many of my novels. It began what is now called the Saga of the Skolian Empire. But for years, it has been one of my hardest stories to find. *Analog* sold out of the issue years ago and I have very few copies left myself.

In November of 2011, when I was the Author Guest of Honor at Windycon in Chicago, ISFiC Press brought out a hardcover anthology of my fiction for the convention. Titled *Aurora in Four Voices*, it included "Light and Shadow." Before I sent this story to them, I went through the text, polishing the prose. I couldn't help but notice that the story had a different feel than my other works in the Ruby Dynasty universe. Less modern. I considered updating it to match the character of the other works, with their glossier tech. But I decided against that change. The feel of "Light and Shadow" matches the time I wrote it, which was even before I finished my first novel, *Primary Inversion*. Also, it takes place at an earlier time in the chronology of the Ruby Dynasty series than most of the other stories. So it seemed fitting to leave the feel of the story as I originally wrote it over two decades ago.

I hope you enjoy reading "Light and Shadow" as much as I enjoyed writing the story.

1

A FLASH OF STARLIGHT

Kelric spoke into the empty air of the cockpit. "Glint Control, I'm ready to give it another go."

"Standby, Glint One Eight." Lieutenant Tyrson's voice came over the audio-com, sounding so clear he could have been right next to Kelric's reclined seat instead of on the ground far below. "Glint One Eight, tracking and instrumentation are go. You're cleared for test procedure four. Calculations indicate your wing stress will be within safe limits."

Safe? An unwelcome thought rose from a hidden corner of Kelric's mind. *So what? You have nothing worth keeping safe.*

He banished the thought back to its dark recess. Then he whipped his plane through a dizzying set of loops and rolls, uncaring of the g forces that pressed him into his seat. He lay more than sat in the tight cockpit, with the computer console and display panels in front of him. Data streamed across the visor of his faceplate, changing so fast to keep up with his maneuvers that it blurred. Holomaps of the planet Diesha turned on his screens, the deserts shaded like orange and red paint mixing on a palette. Isolated mountains broke the land's flatness in convoluted spears, and no clouds showed in a sky so blue it seemed to vibrate.

Kelric pulled out of his last loop and grinned. "How does that read, Lieutenant?

Tyrson chuckled. "Like a dream."

And what a dream, Kelric thought. He was the first pilot to test the Glint-18, a rocket fighter powered by nuclear fusion that made other planes he had flown seem like slugs.

Captain, the Glint's computer thought. *How can a dream read?*

It's just a figure of speech, Kelric answered, directing the reply with more intensity than when his thoughts were for himself only. He touched the valve in his survival suit where the prong on his pilot's seat plugged into his spine. It connected the cyberware built into the plane with the network of fibers implanted in his body. The system created a direct link from his brain to the Glint's onboard systems. His motion was reflexive, a reminder that he was linked to a computer and not a person. He forgot sometimes. The Glint's efforts to learn idioms made it seem self-conscious, like a human being, someone new to a language.

Tyron's voice interrupted his reverie. "Captain Valdoria, I can't access mod four of your computer."

"Checking," Kelric said. To the Glint, he thought, *Run a diagnostic on your fourth mod.* It was a vital mod, one that controlled the extra shielding against heat, ultraviolet radiation, and cosmic rays that the craft needed to survive in orbit. Although this wasn't the first plane Kelric had flown with orbital capability, it far surpassed the others. Today, however, his tests concerned only its performance in a planetary atmosphere.

Lights suddenly blazed across his controls, glowing like holiday decorations. *Altimeter error,* the Glint thought. *Environment control error.*

Tyrson's voice snapped out of the audiocom. "Glint One Eight, your chase planes have lost contact with your—"

As Tyrson's voice cut off, the Glint added, *Audiocom failure.*

Slow down, Kelric told the plane. The rockets fired, but the plane didn't turn, so it sped up instead.

Cockpit pressure dropping, the Glint thought. *I've sealed your survival suit.*

What the hell? *Glint, slow us down.*

Neither the thrusters nor the attitude jets are responding, it answered.

Reboot their control mod.

Reboot successful, Then: *Captain Valdoria, we're approaching escape velocity.*

Kelric stared at the console. To escape the planet's gravitational pull, he had to go over eleven kilometers a second, far faster than he had prepared for on this flight. This was nuts. He couldn't go into space.

A thought stirred in the recesses of his mind: *Why not? You have nothing to lose. Nothing worth keeping.*

The Glint's thought cut through his own: *Do you want to try slowing down again?*

Kelric sat motionless, watching his holomaps. They all showed images of the world below him as it receded in the sable backdrop of space.

If we don't slow down within eight seconds, the Glint thought, *we won't have enough fuel to return to base. In fourteen seconds we won't be able to reach any emergency landing site.*

Kelric's private thoughts whispered like a strain of discordant music playing under the computer's voice: *You can drift in space forever. With the stars as your lovers, you'll never be alone.*

Escape velocity achieved, the Glint thought. *We are leaving the planet.*

With a mental heave, Kelric snapped himself back to reality. *Glint, return to base!*

At first nothing happened. Then the thrusters rumbled in their bay and the rockets fired, flattening him in his seat.

Re-entry initiated, the Glint thought.

Kelric exhaled. *Do we have enough fuel to get back?*

Yes.

So I'm going to live after all. Kelric wasn't sure whether to be grateful or to curse.

"We weren't able to analyze much of your cyber log," General Schuldman said. He was seated behind the darkwood desk in his office, a huge room as spare and as strong as the grey-haired man who used it. "Most of the log was garbled. Do you have any comments to add to our quick-look report?"

Kelric was sitting in front of the desk, uncomfortable in a leather-bound chair. Was Schuldman asking for more details about his hesitation during the flight? Kelric had none; he wasn't certain himself what had happened in that moment when he had let the plane leave the planet. However, that hadn't caused the system failures.

"There's a flaw in the Glint's computer, sir," he said. "I think it's the neural-hardware interface."

Schuldman nodded. "Apparently the computer tried to break the lock that keeps it out of your private thoughts. When your mind blocked it, the system froze up."

His private thoughts. Kelric had enough trouble himself dealing with those; it was no wonder it had confused a computer. "Can the problem be fixed?"

"Our techs repaired the damage," the general said. "Jessa Zaubern checked their work herself. It shouldn't try to break your lock again." He considered Kelric. "Engineering also ran simulations using the higher velocity data you obtained. Their results suggest the Glint may indeed be able to withstand the huge accelerations Dr. Zaubern claimed in her first reports."

So Jessa had been right. It didn't surprise Kelric; she had one hell of a good mind. "Sir, the ship may be able to withstand those accelerations, but the engines can't achieve them."

Schuldman regarded him steadily. "That's why we're putting an inversion engine in it."

What the hell? They wanted to put a *starship* engine in a plane? What a thought.

Schuldman was watching him with a scrutiny that made Kelric wonder if the general questioned his judgment in letting the Glint leave the planet. Probably not. Schuldman had specifically directed him to test the limits of the craft's abilities. As for Kelric's private thoughts during those moments, they were just that. Private.

In any case, putting a starship engine in a plane added a new dimension to the project. Intrigued, Kelric said, "Even data from my last flight can only give us a rough idea of what will happen at higher velocities. I wasn't going fast enough to test the parameters that would affect a starship."

Schuldman considered him. "That's why I'm looking for a volunteer to test the modified aircraft."

Kelric knew the general's ability to get fast results made him one of the most valued officers in the Space Test Wing. The rumor mill also claimed

Schuldman had earned his reputation by pushing his planes—and their pilots—to the limit.

What a ride it would be, though! The speed, the challenge, rushing on the edge—the idea exhilarated Kelric. Then he thought of the risks and sobered up. Neither the Glint nor any other plane he knew was ready to fly with a starship drive.

Unbidden, a thought crept out of the shadows in his mind: *Go ahead. Do it. You have nothing to lose.*

Kelric spoke. "I'd like to volunteer, sir."

Schuldman nodded with approval. "Very well, Captain. The flight will be in three days."

2

ARROYO DAWN

The only light in the sunken living room came from the clock on a table, its violet glow coaxing gleams from the glassy furniture and paneling. Moonlight poured through the big window in the north wall. Outside, the city of Arosa lay under the desert sky, its scattered lights glittering like moonlight trapped in a diamond. It was the only town within a day's hovercar drive of Arosa Space Force Base, an installation isolated so far out in the desert that nothing but an occasional corkscrew cricket lived near enough to see the aircraft tests.

Kelric sat in his dark glossy penthouse, sprawled on the couch, holding a glass of desert honey. He had no idea where the whisky got the name honey. It tasted like cleaning fluid. He grimaced and poured his drink back in the bottle, then clunked the tumbler down on the glass table.

"So," he muttered. "You like sitting here in the dark or what?"

"That's a good question," a woman said.

Kelric jumped to his feet so fast he knocked over his glass. The lights in the room came on, blinding him. As his vision cleared he saw a statuesque woman by the door, a golden figure with an angel's face and masses of radiant curls that floated around her face and spilled down her back.

"For flaming sake, Mother," he growled. "What are you doing here?"

She gave him a wry smile. "I'm glad to see you too."

"You surprised me." She rarely showed up with letting him know first. "How did you get in?"

"You left the door unlocked." She walked over to him, her gold hair tousled around her shoulders. "I thought something was wrong. Then I heard you talking to yourself."

"I wasn't expecting visitors."

Her smile smoothed away the worried furrow that had creased her forehead. "I decided to come after I saw you on the news tonight."

Kelric reddened. He was trying to forget that broadcast. News of his last flight had leaked to the press and a local reporter had called the base to ask if she could interview him. Schuldman gave the go-ahead, unaware that Kelric avoided public speaking like he avoided jumping into hot tar pits. The project information officer had told him to satisfy the press with a good story. Apparently it helped garner public support for the base. So Kelric had tried to prepare for the interview. But when he had walked into the broadcast studio with its bright lights and buzzing crews, it had rattled him so much, he couldn't do much more than mumble yes and no to the reporter's questions.

"That was quite a story," his mother said. "How did they put it? 'The handsome hero of Space Command.'"

"I looked like an idiot."

"Actually, I thought you fit the role of hero well."

He couldn't help but smile. "You would think I was heroic if I fell on my face in the mud."

She chuckled. "You looked every bit the valiant flyer they made you out to be." Her smile faded. "But I know you, Kelric. Something was wrong."

"I hate speaking in public. You know that, too."

"It was more than that."

"I don't know what you're looking for." He picked up the whiskey glass. "Listen, I'm glad to see you. I don't mean to be rude. But I'm tired. I just don't feel like company tonight."

She spoke quietly. "Sitting here alone in the dark won't bring Cory back to life. And committing suicide in your fancy plane won't bring you any closer to her."

He went rigid. "Good night, Mother."

"It's been two months since her funeral." She watched him with those gold eyes that saw far too much. "In that entire time, I've never seen you shed a single tear or heard you say one word about it. You sit up here surrounded by her things and brood. It's not healthy."

His voice tightened. "This is where I live."

"You can change where you live. Find a place that isn't full of memories."

Memories? He didn't even have those. His wife's death had left a void with nothing but his grief to fill it. Why had he married another officer? Losing a friend in battle was hard enough. When the news had come, two months and an eternity ago, that the battlecruiser Cory commanded had been destroyed—and she with it—a part of him had died as well.

Kelric pushed down the memory. He didn't want pity. What could he do to make his well-meaning mother go away before her solicitude started him unraveling?

"I'll look at apartments next week," he said.

Her luminous face lit with a smile. "There's a nice place on Arroyo Cliffs. You could see it Tillsday evening."

"All right." That would be after his test flight of Schuldman's mutant plane with its starship engine.

Dawn's ruddy light stretched long shadows across the red sands. Sunrise turned the airfield crimson and reflected off the Glint's hull like sparks of fire. Out in the desert, nothing but rock spires showed as far as the horizon. Only the rare boom of a snare-drum cactus interrupted the dawn's silent splendor.

Kelric walked around the Glint. The only visible changes were the photon thrusters mounted behind the rocket exhaust. He knew what waited inside that plane, though—a marvel ready to shoot him into the heavens.

Inversion. The word had fascinated him since childhood. At the Academy he had earned his degree in inversion theory, the physics of faster-than-light travel. His people had once believed reaching supraluminal speeds was impossible. It meant going through the speed of light, where slower travelers would see his mass become infinite and his ship rotated until it pointed perpendicular to its true direction. Time for him would stop relative to the rest of the universe. Which of course could never happen. So how could he go faster-than-light?

The answer turned out to be simple.

It depended on imaginary numbers, the square roots of negative numbers. Relativistic physics said his mass and energy became imaginary at supraluminal speeds. If he also added an imaginary part to his speed, the equations no longer blew up at light speed. By venturing into a universe where speed had both real and imaginary parts, he could go *around* light speed like a hovercar leaving the road could go around a tree. But for a starship, "leaving the road" meant leaving the real universe.

Kelric pressed his hand against the plane's hatch. "What do you say, Glint? Want to go faster than a photon?" The plane couldn't of course. It wasn't designed for interstellar travel. But the inversion engine could accelerate it far better than the rockets. Engineering thought he might reach one hundredth the speed of light. It would make his last flight a snail's pace in comparison.

"I just hope they fixed the computer," Kelric said.

"Fixed it, double-checked it, triple-checked it," a woman's gravelly voice said behind him. "Can't have you blowing up out there. You and me got a debt to settle."

Kelric turned to see Jessa Zaubern, a gaunt figure in the blue jumpsuit worn by the engineers assigned to the Glint project. Her close cut cap of fiery hair glistened in the dawn's light.

He snorted. "You're the one who owes me money, Zaub."

Her grin animated her face, chasing away her usual stoicism. "Next game, I'm going to wipe your bank account clean."

Kelric smiled. He and Jessa got along well. He was one of the few people she let see the sentimental streak under her gruffness. They understood each other, both of them plagued by the same awkwardness with words. He was also the only person who had ever beat her at Dieshan choker slam, a game invented by the base's notorious circle of card players. And she was a better engineer than card player. If she had triple-checked his plane, it was in good shape.

Jessa surveyed the Glint. "The fusion rockets will get you off planet." She slanted a gaze at him. "You can use the inversion engine once you're in orbit. You got positron fuel."

"I don't know, Zaub. Positrons for a plane?" He grinned his challenge. "It'll never work."

"Like hell, Kelly boy." She banged her palm on the Glint's hull. "We used EM fields to suspend the fuel in a canister. You fire the thrusters, a defect in the fields leak positrons into the beambox, same as in a starship."

Even after his briefing, Kelric had trouble imagining the plane carrying an inversion selector and beambox. The wheel-shaped selector culled electrons out of the cosmic ray flux in space, letting only those with highest energies enter the mirrored beambox. Once inside, the electrons annihilated with positrons, creating ultra high energy photons that reflected out the thrusters.

"Just as long as it does what it's supposed to do," he said.

Jessa peered at him. "You really think it has a problem?"

Did he? "I'll only be carrying a hundred kilograms of positrons."

"That's more than you need. It's not like you're going anywhere." She shrugged. "Hell, one gram of positrons makes a million billion billion annihilations. That's a lot of push."

"I suppose." He tilted his head towards the Glint. "So you really think she can reach one percent of light speed?"

"Should," Jessa said. "We don't have enough data at higher velocities to know for sure."

Interesting. "You mean you don't know its top speed?"

Jessa scowled at him. "Don't even *think* it."

He regarded her innocently. "Think what?"

"You be careful with my plane."

He laughed amiably. "I'm going to wreak havoc on it."

"Very funny." Her voice quieted. "You be careful with Kelric, too."

"Hell, he'll be fine. He's only an idiot when reporters interview him."

"I'm not joking." Jessa shook her head. "People look at you, they see big and quiet. They don't think you feel. They don't think you think."

He shifted his weight. "It doesn't bother me."

"Kelric, listen." She came over to him. "You're smarter than all of them put together. And you feel. Too much. You keep thinking and feeling and locking it up. It will eat holes in your heart."

Where the hell had that come from? "I'm fine."

Jessa put her hands on her hips. "Only one dumb thing I've ever seen you do. And that's agreeing to take up this plane. Schuldman had no right to push you into this mission."

"He didn't push me. I volunteered."

"Yeah, right." She poked her finger at his chest. "I want my plane back in one piece."

"It's not your plane, Zaub."

"Just remember what I said."

He did his best to look reassuring. "All right."

"Good." She paused awkwardly. "Good luck."

Kelric smiled. "Thanks."

After Jessa left, Kelric climbed into the cockpit and ran more tests. He put the computer through every one of its routines and it answered without a glitch.

Although the Glint could take off vertically, today Kelric tested it on the runway. After Tyrson gave him clearance, he sped down the asphalt and soared into the air, exulting in acceleration pushing him against his seat. He loved that sensation of speed.

As he shot higher into the sky, the world of Diesha spread out on his screens in a desolate landscape of sunrise colors. He accelerated steadily and the Glint answered like an extension of his own body. The wings folded back against the fuselage, cutting drag and preparing for the supersonic shock wave. Mach 1, Mach 2, Mach 4. Finally he hit the speed where the computer had developed jitters during his last flight.

"Glint One Eight to Control," Kelric said. "Systems look good here."

"I read the same," Tyrson said over the audiocom.

"Good." Kelric grinned. "I'm going to give it a kick."

Captain, the Glint thought. *I don't think kicking me will serve any purpose.*

Kelric chuckled. *Don't worry. It's just another idiom.* He fired the rockets, breathing in grunts to keep from blacking out from the g-forces. Mach 8, 16, 32. He hit escape velocity and kept going. On his screens, Diesha changed from a flat landscape to curved globe studded with ruby deserts.

"She's beautiful," he murmured.

Tyrson chuckled. "Is that someone you see up there or are you thinking about your last date?"

"Lady Diesha," Kelric said. *Beautiful sorceress,* he thought. *Hold me in your arms until the pain stops.*

We've cleared the planet, the Glint announced. *Do you want to start the inversion engine?*

Let's give it a go. Kelric fired the photon thrusters—and went into quasis.

Without quantum stasis, more commonly known as quasis, he would have died. A starship engine could accelerate a craft up to thousands of times the force of gravity, which would have smeared him all over his seat if he hadn't had protection. The waveform modulators in the quasis coil worked on an atomic level, keeping the quantum wavefunction of the ship from changing state. During quasis, nothing could alter the configuration of particles in the plane or anything it carried, including him; on a macroscopic level, the craft became a rigid solid that no force could deform. Only the atomic clock that limited their quasis time was unaffected. Kelric felt nothing; the only way he knew he hadn't been conscious the entire time was by the sudden jump in speed on his display.

Tyrson's voice burst out of the audiocom. "Captain, she's working like a dream!"

"You bet," Kelric said. *Thanks, Zaub,* he thought. He fired the thrusters again and his speed suddenly read three thousand kilometers per second.

"Glint Control," Kelric said. "I'm at one percent of light speed."

"We read you smooth as silk," Tyrson said. "It's beautiful."

An unwelcome thought came to his mind. *No, it's empty. Everything is empty.* He pushed the thought away and spoke into the audiocom. "I'm going to crank it up again."

Another voice came on the com. "Captain, this is General Schuldman. Your systems are operating well, better than predicted. The decision to exceed this speed is yours, but if you do so you will be going against the advice of the team that installed your engine. Do you understand?"

Kelric knew Schuldman wanted him to push the Glint's limit. He also knew the general meant to make sure he knew the risks. "Understood, sir."

He fired the photon thrusters. A vibration shook through the ship, a gentle shaking but one that didn't feel right.

"Captain!" Static crackled in Tyrson's voice. "I'm reading you at ten percent of light speed."

"Captain Valdoria." Schuldman's voice came through the static. "That's fast enou—"

Kelric fired the thrusters before the general finished; that way, he wasn't disobeying orders. The display jumped to one hundred thousand kilometers per second. He hit the thrusters again and the number doubled. He was going at two-thirds the speed of light.

A voice on his audiocom drawled. "Are you recei . . . return to base . . ." The words faded away.

For a moment Kelric had no idea who had spoken. Then he realized it was Schuldman. *Glint,* he thought. *What's wrong with the audiocom?*

It can't cope with the time dilation.

Interesting. Starship audiocoms easily compensated for the effect of relativistic speeds on radio waves, but the Glint had no reason to carry one. He wasn't supposed to be going anywhere near this fast.

How long does Control think we've been gone? Kelric asked.

Thirty-three minutes, the Glint answered. *My clock says thirty minutes have passed for us.*

How about that? We jumped three minutes into the future. When he went this fast, Control recorded his clock as running slow. However, he recorded the clocks on Diesha as running slow. It was like when he sat in a magtrain and it looked like the train next to him was going backward when in fact his train was the one that had started to move forward. Relative to him, the other train *was* going backward. Similarly, relative to this plane, Diesha was shooting off in the other direction. Only when he turned the Glint around did it break the symmetry of their relative motion. What it meant was that when he returned home, he would be several minutes younger than everyone at the base.

Captain. The Glint's urgency cut through his mind. *The strain on this craft exceeds advised safety limits.*

No one ever claimed this job was safe, Kelric thought. *How fast can you go, sweet Glint?* Fast enough to the blow the grief out of his heart? Could anything take him that fast, that high, that far?

I also register a strain in your mind greater than advisable safety limits, the Glint said.

Who programmed you to tell me that? Jessa Zaubern?

Captain, I advise that we return to base.

Kelric watched his visored reflection in the console. *Can we invert?*

You mean go faster than the speed of light?

That's right.

Captain, this flight wasn't set up for such a maneuver.

Just answer the question.

I don't know if we can invert, the Glint thought. *But if we do, we won't have enough fuel to get home.*

Raise the beambox threshold. By scooping up only higher energy electrons, he could get more bang out of each annihilation and extend the range of his positron fuel.

If I raise it, the Glint answered, *you will run out of air before we find enough electrons with an energy that high. You will die.*

So invert the fuel first.

I see no reason to—

The cosmic ray flux is higher in supraluminal space, Kelric thought. *We'll find electrons a lot faster there.*

They will be there and we will be here, the Glint said. *Photons produced by annihilations in imaginary space do us no good in real space.*

Sure they will, Kelric thought. *If I release a flock of birds by an open window, some are bound to fly through it. As long as the engine operates here, some photons will invert back here.*

That violates energy conservation.

For flaming sake. His computer was arguing with him. *No, it doesn't. What we gain, imaginary space loses.*

Photons are not birds. Now the Glint sounded like Jessa. *Inversion engines are not windows.*

Just do it, Kelric thought.

Captain, you may not survive this procedure.

Are you refusing to accept my commands?

Yes.

Kelric frowned. *You can't do that.*

What you suggest could be fatal. It amounts to throwing away your fuel.

The hell it does.

The only way for imaginary photons to become real, the Glint thought, *is for their existence quantum number to change from zero to one. That doesn't happen spontaneously.*

So what? Kelric answered. *Nothing spontaneously inverts. If starship engines can force starships to do it, they ought to work on photons, too.*

There was a long pause. Then the Glint said, *A finite probability exists that you are correct and that this either brilliant or insane idea of yours may actually work. If it works, it will revolutionize star travel.*

I'm a test pilot, Kelric thought. *I'm supposed to test things.*

You are putting yourself in too much danger.

Yes, I have a dangerous job. That doesn't mean I shouldn't do it.

I still advise against the procedure. The Glint's thought came with what felt like genuine reluctance. *However, it appears I am unable to refuse your command.*

Good. Kelric glanced over his displays. *Reset the engine to invert its fuel in increments of point one percent.*

Engine reset.

Kelric fired the photon thrusters—and his speed jumped to ninety-eight percent of light. The stars leapt on his holomap, converging towards a point in front of the plane. Data flashed on his displays: if Control could still track him, they would read his length as shrunk by 80 percent and his mass increased by five hundred percent.

Why didn't we invert? Kelric asked.

We need to get closer to light speed, the Glint told him.

Starships manage from a lot slower speeds than this.

Starships have entire systems dedicated to optimizing their inversion capability, the Glint thought. *I don't.*

Kelric knew he should return to the base before time dilation jumped him any farther into the future. He had already gained more than half an hour. But he couldn't make himself turn around. Up here he could speed away from the grief, the loneliness, the huge emptiness.

This time when he fired the thrusters, his display leapt to 99.999999 percent of light speed. His mass increased by a factor of seven thousand. The starlight turned into x-rays. In one minute, five days passed on Diesha.

We still can't invert, the Glint thought.

Kelric fired the thrusters again. Centuries passed on Diesha. Now they were all dead. All of them. Everyone he had ever loved.

Cory, I can't do it, he thought. *I can't live in a universe where the people I love are gone.*

No inversion achieved, the Glint thought.

Kelric gritted his teeth and fired the thrusters—

—and the universe turned inside out, yanking him with it, his body and mind twisting like a tortured Möbius strip.

3

BEYOND THE END

The agonizing sensation stopped as abruptly as it had begun. The stars reappeared, their colors returned to normal but their positions inverted through a point that appeared to be infinitely far in front of the plane. Kelric recognized none of the eerily distorted constellations.

We inverted, the Glint thought. *But it definitely wasn't as smooth as silk.*

Kelric drew in a deep breath. *You're learning your idioms.* That was like no inversion he had ever experienced. He didn't know if he could survive it a second time.

I need you to specify a path in spacetime, the Glint said. *We're supraluminal.*

He struggled to clear his mind. Time and space switched character at faster than light speeds. Now he couldn't back up in space but he *could* back up in time. The relativistic equations allowed him to go into the past. A sublight observer would see an anti-matter Glint flying backwards from its destination to its origin. If he worked it right, he could compensate for his time-dilated leap into the future by leaping into the past here.

If only he could go back to before Cory died.

Unfortunately, no matter how much he wanted it, the final result of his trip couldn't violate reality. A thousand pilots before him had verified that law of physics. The best he could do with a starship was come home with the same amount of time passing there as for him. With the Glint, he would be lucky to come out anywhere near the day when he had left Diesha. This morning. Except now it was centuries, even millennia in the past.

His displays weren't telling him anything. The inversion had scrambled them. *Glint, how fast are we going?*

One trillion times the speed of light.

WHAT?

One trillion ti—

Slow down!

Silence.

Kelric blinked at the gibberish on his displays. *Did anything happen?*

We slowed to one hundred thirty-two percent light speed.

How did we get going so fast before?

When we passed light speed, our mass decreased, the Glint thought. *So we sped up, which made our mass decrease, which sped us up, which—*

I get the idea. To himself only, shutting the Glint out of his mind, Kelric thought, *Can you imagine a more spectacular way to die? Hurtle along at infinite speed with zero mass and infinite length, your body turning to dust while time stops for the rest of the Universe?*

And then what? he asked himself. *You think Cory will be waiting? You think she'll open her arms wide, welcoming you for the stupidity of killing yourself?* He could see her glaring at him, her dark hair whipping in an imaginary wind.

"Cory, I miss you," Kelric murmured.

I don't understand 'Cory,' the Glint thought.

I never did either, Kelric admitted. *But gods, I loved her.* To the image of Cory in his mind, he thought, *Good-bye, my love.* Then he took a deep breath and directed his thoughts outward, focusing them enough so they would reach the computer. *Glint, figure out a course that will get us home as near to when we left as possible.* He gave voice to the realization lifting above his grief like a bird in flight. *If there's a way to get back alive, I want to do it.*

I'll do my best, Captain. After a pause, the Glint thought, *I'm ready.*

Kelric fired the thrusters. The stars shifted position, but nothing else changed. He fired them again, trying not to dwell on how little fuel he had left. The stars collapsed into a point, their sluggish photons lumbering towards him as he leapt farther and farther into the past. He fired the thrusters—

And ripped in two.

Kelric snapped like a rubber band pulled too far too fast, its torn edges writhing in space, screaming, screaming . . .

Suddenly he was whole again. He felt ill, dizzy, disoriented, as if his body had reset.

"We inverted," the Glint said.

Kelric swallowed. *Why did it feel so strange?* After a moment he realized the Glint had used the com instead of their neural link. He spoke out loud. "What happened?"

"The top of the plane, including the top of your body, inverted two picoseconds before the rest of the craft."

Good gods. "Am I normal now?"

"Essentially."

"What do you mean, 'essentially'?"

"Only 99.99 percent of your mass reinverted."

"What didn't come back?"

"The missing molecules are distributed throughout the lower half of your body." Then the Glint added, "We gave it a go and most of us went."

Kelric managed a wan laugh, trying to ignore his bizarre mental image of 0.01 percent of his body doomed to forever hurtle into the past. "What happened to my cyber link with you?"

"The reinversion scrambled it."

"Can we still get home?"

"Yes. However, we no longer have enough fuel to slow down."

"Raise the beambox threshold again," Kelric said. "Then do the bit with inverting the fuel."

"We still won't collect enough before you run out of air and suffocate."

That was it? He had almost made it back only to find he couldn't stop? He couldn't accept that. "There has to be a way to get home."

"Getting home is easy," the Glint said, "But when we arrive you will be dead."

Kelric grimaced. "You're encouraging."

"What do you want me to do?"

He touched the spare tank on his survival suit. "Can you tap my emergency air reserve?"

"I already have."

Kelric sat absorbing his situation. Then he snapped his fingers. "I don't breathe in quasis."

"This is true."

"So crank up the beambox threshold and put me in quasis until we reach Diesha."

"It is inadvisable to your survival to remain in quasis that long."

"Dying isn't advisable to my survival either," Kelric said. "What's the problem with quasis?"

"It prevents the arrangement of molecules in your body from adapting as your environment changes. If you stay in too long, your environment will change too much. When you come out, your molecular wave function may not be able to readjust without catastrophic fluctuations."

Catastrophic who? "Meaning what, exactly?"

"Every atom in your body is hit with a force when you come out of quasis," the Glint said. "It's because your environment has changed. And those forces aren't necessarily in the same directions. The more your environment changes, the bigger the discrepancies. Go too long, and it could tear you apart atom by atom."

Not exactly how he had planned to end the day. "You're my environment," he pointed out. "And you go into stasis, too. That means you can't change. So neither does my environment. In theory." Of course, theories usually described an ideal case, which was far from what they had here.

"That might protect you," the Glint said. "However, it doesn't protect me."

"Your environment can't change *that* much. We're in interstellar space."

"Space is far from a true vacuum," the Glint said. "And it won't take much to make the plane collapse. Its structure is already strained past its safety limits."

A solution had to exist. Every problem had an answer. He just needed to think of it. "Can you set the timer to bring us out at periodic intervals?" Kelric asked. "Do it before our time in stasis becomes too long. We'd only need an instant to readjust. I probably wouldn't even be conscious."

The Glint went silent, and Kelric could almost feel it calculating. Finally it said, "There is a great deal of uncertainty associated with this procedure."

Kelric thought of the shadows in his mind. Damn it, he *wanted* to get better. "I'll take uncertain life over certain death."

"I understand, Captain."

"So let's do it."

After a pause, the Glint said, "Ready."

Kelric fired the photon thrusters . . .

Nausea surged over Kelric and he almost lost the breakfast he had eaten a few hours and who knew how long ago. His forward screen showed Diesha swelling into view like a ruby and turquoise jewel. They weren't close enough to land, however.

He struggled to clear his thoughts. "Glint? Why did you wake me up?"

"We're going to disintegrate. I thought you would want to know."

Hell and damnation! "Get us down as far as you can before the plane falls apart."

"Re-entry initiated. I've activated my emergency beacon."

Kelric wondered if they had returned to a time when anyone existed to pick up that beacon. "Can the reactor's shielding survive the crash?"

"Yes."

So at least they wouldn't splatter a nuclear reactor all over the landscape. He hoped the same was true for him. The Glint, designed to be as light as possible, didn't carry an escape capsule to protect him when he ejected. "Will you be able to slow down enough for me to eject?"

"I calculate a fifty-three percent probability that you will survive ejection."

Well, that was better than zero. Even if he didn't make it, at least the Glint's mind would survive. The computer was better shielded even than the reactor.

Kelric touched the console. "Jessa and her team will have you fixed up in no time."

"I don't think that will be possible," The Glint sounded subdued.

"Why not?"

"When we reinverted, I created a cybershell for your mind. It damaged my systems."

"A what shell?"

"Cybershell. I ran your brain as a subprocess of my own. Your mind wouldn't have survived reinversion otherwise,"

Kelric whistled. "That's impossible."

"Not completely. However, it did leave me unprotected during reinversion. It corrupted my systems. By the time we crash, my functions and memory will be degraded past recovery."

No, Kelric thought. "You killed yourself so I could live."

"I'm only a computer."

"A computer, yes." He spoke quietly. "But 'only'? I would never use that word for you."

"Captain, thank you." Then it said, "We're disintegrating."

"I won't forget what you did for me," Kelric said.

"Take care." With just the barest pause, the Glint added, "Let yourself heal, Kelric."

The plane ejected him.

Kelric went out the top, shooting upwards as the Glint fell away from him in pieces. Windblast buffeted him so roughly that he almost blacked out.

He began to fall. Tucking his chin to his chest, he held his legs together and crossed his arms while he tumbled through the air. Silence surrounded him and clouds covered the landscape. He tried to look at the altimeter on his arm, but the numbers blurred. It took his groggy brain a moment to comprehend that he had used up the air in his emergency tank. He clawed at his helmet, his fingers scraping across the face plate. Darkness closed around him, warm, inviting . . .

A blast of cold air slapped Kelric awake. His helmet had opened and his suit timer was going off, triggering the release of a parachute. It jerked him so hard, it felt as if his arms would rip off his shoulders.

Mercifully, the buffeting soon eased. His survival kit deployed, its life raft dangling from his suit like seaweed waving in an ocean of air. Clouds closed around him and he fell through a wet mist that ate away at his sense of up and down, right and left.

Gradually Kelric realized the world wasn't silent. A rumble throbbed below him. As he fell through the fog, the growl swelled into the roar of waves hitting land. Even when he sealed his helmet, he heard the thundering voice.

He had no warning before he hit water. He plunged into it, his limbs tangling in the parachute's suspension lines. As he struggled to free himself, he plowed into sand. With a huge kick he shot out of the water, breathing the few moments of borrowed air in his suit.

Kelric pulled free of the parachute and grabbed the life raft. He had run out of air, but when he opened his face plate, a wave smashed into him. Another wave came, another, and another. The breakers tore away the life raft and rolled him over and over, his lungs straining while he struggled not to gulp in water. If he didn't get air soon, he would pass out.

His feet scraped the bottom for only an instant, but it was enough. He shoved against the sand and shot upwards, clearing the breakers long enough to gasp in a breath. Then he was back in the water, fighting the waves. He touched sand again, again, and again, and then he was stumbling up a sandy slope, waves crashing around him in frothy turbulence.

Kelric staggered onto the beach, wading out of the mist into watery sunlight. Ahead of him, a hill slanted up to a road—where a hovervan with flashing red lights was braking to a stop. As people jumped out of the vehicle, engines rumbled overhead. He looked up to see a flyer circling, its military insignia gleaming in the sunlight.

A woman in a blue jumpsuit ran toward him, her shoulder-length hair glinting like copper. As Kelric sunk to his knees in the sand, people surrounded him. The woman knelt in front of him, tears on her face. "You crazy man."

Kelric barely managed to croak out an answer. "Zaub? How did your hair grow so fast?"

"Six months you've been gone." Her voice shook. "Six months we've been thinking your hide was finished."

"I came back to get the money you owed me."

She pulled him into her arms. "Welcome home."

Kelric hugged her back, unable to respond as silent tears ran down his face.

The broadcasts that aired following his return made him out to be a bigger-than-life hero. Over and over they showed the scene of his parents embracing him, the son they thought they had lost, his breathtakingly beautiful mother with tears streaming down her golden face. Space Command took advantage of the good public relations and paraded him around in his uniform, keeping quiet about that fact that they also took him off flight status and sent him to a therapist. Kelric went where they told him to go, stood where they told him to stand, and endeavored not to look like an idiot.

All the reports went on with great enthusiasm about the dramatic moment when he wept on the beach for the joy of seeing home. Kelric let them say what they wanted. He knew the truth, deep inside where suppressed grief had once crippled his heart.

Those healing tears had been for Cory.

A POETRY

OF

ANGLES

AND

DREAMS

1

SPACES OF THE IMAGINATION

The first time I heard about Riemann surfaces, I fell in love with the subject. It was during a course in applied math for physics majors that I took as an undergraduate. I was intimidated by the course but it also looked intriguing, so I gave it a try.

I adored that class.

To this day, applied math remains my favorite subject. Give me an equation to solve and I'm happy. This essay describes some of the ways I've incorporated math into my stories. I've started out with a few equations for those who enjoy them, but it isn't necessary to understand those to follow the rest of the essay. I've also included analogies and pictures I hope will elucidate the beautiful concepts behind the mathematics.

My introduction to Riemann sheets came about in that long-ago math class when we delved into the subject of complex analysis, or the math of complex numbers, a subject seen by students of all ages, from preteens first learning about imaginary numbers to doctoral candidates studying theoretical physics. So what is a complex number? We can call it z, where

$$z = x + iy.$$

Here x and y are real numbers, that is, numbers such as 42, 3.64, 84/7 or π. However, *i* is a different beast altogether; it's an imaginary number, specifically the square root of −1:

$$i = \sqrt{-1}.$$

So *z* has a "real part" equal to *x* and an "imaginary part" equal to *y*. We can plot a complex number on what is called the *z*-plane. It looks the same as the *x-y* coordinate plane, except the *x* axis corresponds to the real part of the complex number and the *y* axis corresponds to the imaginary part. On such a graph, the coordinates $(x, y) = z$ give the complex number.

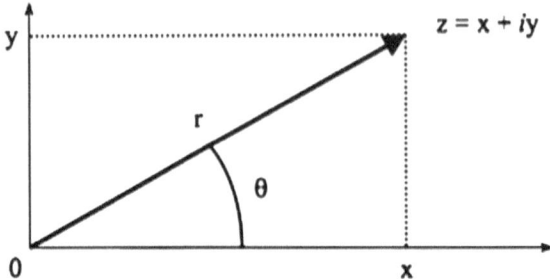

Figure 1: The tip of the arrow gives the complex number z = x + iy, where x is the real part and y is the imaginary part.

We can also represent z by *polar coordinates*. Its position is again given by two numbers, but in this case the two numbers are r and θ, as shown in figure 1. The line drawn from the origin to z has length r and the angle it makes with the x axis is θ. Polar coordinates and x-y coordinates are related; $x = r \cos \theta$, and $y = r \sin \theta$. So

$$z = r \,(\cos \theta + i \sin \theta) = re i\theta.$$

The term $ei\theta = \cos \theta + i \sin \theta$ is called the complex *exponential function*, which often shows up in physics classes, where it has bedeviled many generations of incipient young scientists. The value of r doesn't really matter in these discussions, so to make life easier, I'll set $r = 1$. The angle θ can still vary. In fact, if we let it increase from 0 to 2π, the point z will move in a circle around the x-y plane and come back to where it started.

Imagine that the line from the origin to z is the hour hand on a clock, with z at its tip. When the hand moves once around the clock face, that's analogous to θ moving through a total angle of 2π. After twelve hours, midnight until noon, the hand is back where it started. Go around a second time and the hour goes from noon to midnight. The hours in the first go-around have the same numbers as in the second one, but refer to different times. Go around a third time, though, and we're back to the morning hours.

The convention in math, however, is that $\theta = 0$ when z is on the positive x-axis, which corresponds to an hour hand at 3 o'clock. When z is on the positive y-axis ($\theta = \pi/2$), that corresponds to the hour hand at 12, which means $\theta = \pi/2$ at midnight or noon. Also, in math the convention is that θ increases as z goes counter-clockwise around the plane. If z goes clockwise, θ *decreases* from 0 to $-\pi$ when the time goes from 3 am to 3 pm (or 3 pm to 3 am). The discussion is essentially the same, however, regardless of whether or not we have a minus in front of the angles, and we can just as easily go from 3 am to 3 pm as from midnight to noon. The important part of the analogy is that going once around the clock face corresponds to z moving through a total angle of 2π. So in that sense, z is analogous to a clock.

Something amazing occurs when we take $\sqrt{z}$, the square root of z. Let's check it out. We write

$$\sqrt{z} = z1/2 = ei\theta/2 = \cos(\theta/2) + i\sin(\theta/2).$$

What happens now if the "hour hand" moves clockwise? When θ goes all the way around the clock, $\sqrt{z}$ only makes it halfway around because it depends on $\theta/2$. To see what that means, we'll look at $\theta = -\pi$, which corresponds to 9 o'clock. For that angle,

$$\sqrt{z} = \cos(-\pi/2) + i\sin(-\pi/2) = -i.$$

If we go around the clock once (say 9 am to 9 pm), the angle θ changes by -2π, which means $\theta = -3\pi$ (since we started at $\theta = -\pi$). That's also 9 o'clock. So if $\sqrt{z}$ were well-behaved, it would have the same value at -3π as it did at $-\pi$. However, instead we get

$$\sqrt{z} = \cos(-3\pi/2) + i\sin(-3\pi/2) = i.$$

The square root has different values for $-\pi$ and -3π even though $-\pi$ and -3π are in exactly the same place, the same "hour." So is $\sqrt{z} = i$ or $-i$ at 9 o'clock? It's ambiguous. That's why double-valued functions aren't allowed; z must be unique at every point to be a valid function.

You might wonder what happens if we go around a third time. Is $\sqrt{z}$ triple-valued? Quadruple valued? Where does it stop? As it turns out, the third go-around gives $\sqrt{z} = -i$ again and a fourth gives $\sqrt{z} = i$. So $\sqrt{z}$ alternates between only two values. Unfortunately, even two is too many. In our universe, the math that describes physics requires single-valued quantities. They give unambiguous results; otherwise, we wouldn't know which number to use. But terms like $\sqrt{z}$ come up all the time in the equations of physics. So we seem to be stuck.

The solution to this conundrum is an elegant idea developed by the mathematician Bernhard Riemann in the nineteenth century. Instead of one x-y plane, he suggested stacking two of them together. The top plane, or "sheet," is where z has its first value, and the bottom is for its second value. To go from one sheet to another, we slit them from the origin out to infinity. That slit is called a *branch cut*. If we connect the sheets at their branch cuts, we can go around the top sheet once and then slip through the cut to the bottom sheet for the second time around. Then back to the top sheet. That allows $\sqrt{z}$ to have one value on the top and a different one on the bottom.

Voila! The function is no longer double-valued. The ambiguity goes away as long as we know which sheet we're on. It's like stacking two clocks. The hour hand goes around from 3 am to 3 pm on the top clock, then slides through the branch cut and goes around the second clock from 3 pm to 3 am. Then back to the top clock.

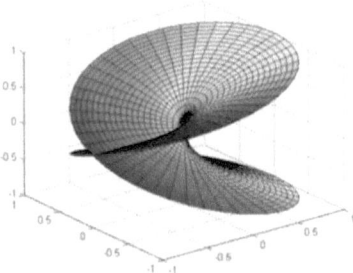

Figure 2: Riemann sheets for √z. This shows curved surfaces, which are hardly clock-like. However, the sheets can be flattened, more like disks. Author: Elb2000.

The square root of z is the simplest case of Riemann sheets. If we have a cube root, we need three sheets; a quartic root requires four sheets, and so on for more complicated functions. However, the basic concept remains the same: the sheets create alternate versions of the complex plane.

As a student, I was fascinated by all this math; as a science fiction writer, I was delighted. What a great way to describe alternate universes! Put them on different Riemann sheets. In "The Spacetime Pool," the character Janelle stumbles through a branch cut that drops her into an alternate reality. In my novel Catch the Lightning, the fighter pilot Althor is thrown through a rip in the Riemann sheet of his universe when his ship is sabotaged.

The seeds of these ideas in my stories go back to when I was trying to think of a fictional faster-than-light drive that was at least mathematically plausible. I figured out that making speed complex in the equations of special relativity would do away with the singularity at the speed of light. Of course, it's a math game; we know of no physical way to make our speed complex. But the math is pretty, so I wrote a paper about it for The American Journal of Physics titled "Complex Speeds and Special Relativity," which appeared in volume 64, the April 1996 issue.

The theory of special relativity developed by Einstein describes what happens if we travel at close to the speed of light. It includes a function called "gamma" that depends on a square root involving v, the speed. If v is complex, the question of Riemann sheets comes up. At least two would be involved and probably more, maybe even an infinite number. When v is complex, the theory also predicts other wonderfully eerie effects. I've used ideas based on that for many stories, including Primary Inversion, my first published novel, and "Light and Shadow," the novelette in this collection. It's been fascinating to play with such fictional extrapolations of the math.

2

A HARMONY OF ARCHES

"The Spacetime Pool" also draws on another of my favorite topics, Fourier analysis. I imagined the Fourier Hall in that story as a great room filled with arches. That idea grew out of my research for another book, *The Veiled Web*, which takes place in Morocco. In doing my research, I fell in love with the gorgeous architecture of Spanish Andalusia and North Africa. I spent hours reading books filled with glossy color pictures of those exquisite buildings. I was also captivated by the repeating nature of the arches, such as in the mosque-cathedral below:

Figure 3: Mezquita de Córdoba, the Cathedral-Mosque of Cordoba, also known as the Catedral de Nuestra Señora de la Asunción. Author: Steven J. Dunlop, Nerstrand, MN.

Fourier analysis is used to model periodic functions, so I wondered if it would work for the arches. First I needed a periodic equation to model the arches. A logical choice is the sine function, which is a repeating wave. However, such a wave oscillates between positive and negative values, and arches are only positive. So I squared the sine waves to make them positive everywhere. Summing several sine waves with different wavelengths gave me a reasonable approximation to the arches, with the cut-off values on the x-axis as shown below:

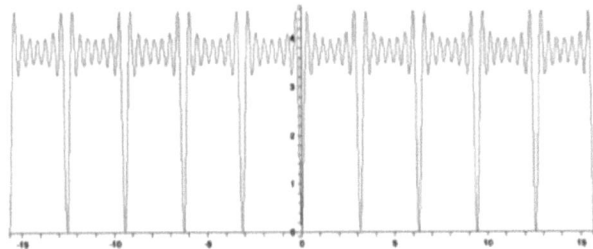

Figure 4: Mathematical model of Moorish arches created by summing sinusoidal functions.

Fourier methods can analyze a signal that repeats in time, say an AC current at sixty cycles per second. If we Fourier transform the signal, we get a new function that depends on frequency instead of time. That new function picks out which frequencies contribute to the signal. For the example with AC current, the transform would give a single line at sixty cycles per second. Most functions aren't that simple; more than one frequency contributes to their shape.

Decomposing a function into frequencies is like breaking down a musical chord into its individual notes. Each note has a specific frequency; put them together and they create the harmonic sound we call a chord. Similarly, a Fourier transform decomposes a function into individual terms that each oscillate at a different frequency.

We can also do the transform backward, that is, take a function that depends on frequency and transform it into one that indicates which times contribute most to the function. In "The Spacetime Pool," Janelle transforms the arches of the Fourier Hall into the time domain. I was curious to see what would happen with that transform, so I did it on my sinusoidal arches and obtained this plot:

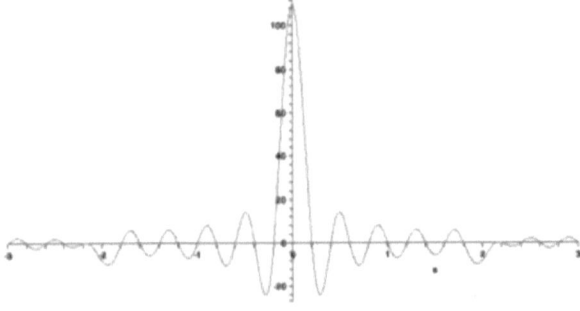

Figure 5: Fourier transform of mathematical model for Moorish arches..

That big peak specifies a time that dominates the rest of the function. The question in the story is then, What does that time mean? "The Spacetime Pool" is actually the first of several stories I plan to write that revolves around the secrets hidden by that enigmatic Fourier Hall.

In my novella "Aurora in Four Voices," the Fourier Fount uses individual fountains to mimic the frequency terms in a Fourier series. Each color of the lights bathing the Fount has a specific frequency that corresponds to one of the fountains. When all those graceful arches of water turn on at once, they create a periodic wave bathed in a sparkling rainbow of light. Of course, fountaining water can't behave literally like a sum of Fourier terms, but I would love to see what such a fountain would look like. The closest I could find in pictures was the Ballagio Fountain in Las Vegas, Nevada.

Using math ideas in my fiction is an aspect of writing I find particularly satisfying. It allows me to blend two of my favorite subjects—math and writing—and create something new.

Figure 6: Bellagio Fountains in Las Vegas.
Author: Jon Sullivan.

ABOUT THE AUTHOR

Catherine Asaro is the author of thirty books, ranging from thrillers to science fiction and fantasy. Her novel *The Quantum Rose* and novella *The Spacetime Pool* both won the Nebula Award, and she has been nominated for multiple Hugo Awards. Asaro holds a doctorate in chemical physics from Harvard; her research specializes in applying the mathematical methods of physics to problems in quantum physics and chemistry

Asaro has appeared as a speaker at many institutions, including the Library of Congress, Georgetown's Communication, Culture, and Technology program, the New Zealand National ConText Writer's program, the Global Competitiveness Forum in Saudi Arabia, and the US Naval Academy. She has been the guest of honor at science fiction conventions across the United States and abroad, including the National Science Fiction Conventions of both Denmark and New Zealand, and served as president for the Science Fiction and Fantasy Writers of America. She can be reached at www.catherineasaro.net and has a Patreon page at www.patreon.com/CatherineAsaro.

CATHERINE ASARO

FROM OPEN ROAD MEDIA

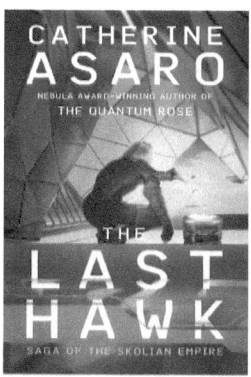
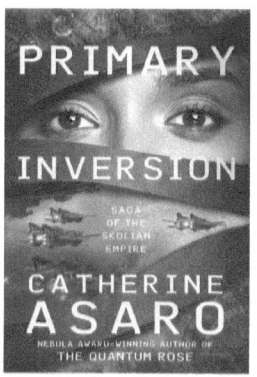
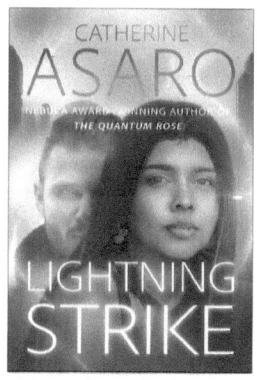

OPEN ROAD

INTEGRATED MEDIA

OPEN ROAD

INTEGRATED MEDIA

Find a full list of our authors and
titles at www.openroadmedia.com

FOLLOW US
@OpenRoadMedia